# POST OFFICE

Charles Bukowski

Introduction by Niall Griffiths

Published by Virgin Books 2009

6 8 10 9 7

First published in Great Britain in 1980 by Melbourne House (Publishers) Ltd.

First published by Virgin Books Ltd in 1992

Published by arrangement with Ecco, an imprint of Harper Collins Publishers, Inc.
New York, New York USA

Virgin Books
Random House, 20 Vauxhall Bridge Road
London SW1V 2SA

www.virginbooks.com
www.randomhouse.co.uk

Addresses for companies within The Random House Group Limited can be found at:
www.randomhouse.co.uk

The Random House Group Limited Reg. No. 954009

A CIP catalogue record for this book is available from the British Library

ISBN 9780753518168

# Introduction

## By Niall Griffiths

It wasn't so much the work itself that was getting to me as the people I had to work alongside. With the work, well, you could just switch off, go onto automatic pilot, let your mind drift and dance as your hands and arms went through the robotic motions; scoop the letters out of the central trough onto the conveyor belt that ran at crotch-height, place parcels and outsize packages into the pigeon-holes at face-height. Brainless and easy, albeit mind-numbingly boring after several hours. But the people, God, my fellow workers ... one would shout 'ah yip! ah yip!' in a high-pitched screech whenever another sack of mail was emptied into the trough; one would call his workmates over to stand and point and snigger if I looped the sacks incorrectly onto the brackets; another kept shaving his head for charity ('do anything for the kiddies, me') and made sure that everyone else knew about it; and, when I fortuitously found a letter addressed to myself out of the many hundreds in the trough and suspected that it was an urgently-needed cheque and asked the boss if I could take it home rather than wait the three days for it to be delivered, he looked at me as if I'd just asked him for permission to expose myself to a nun. 'How do I know it's for you?' 'Because it's got my name on.' 'Could be for someone else with the same name.' 'What, at the same address?' 'How do I know it's your address?' 'Because it's on the form I filled in for you when I started here. Go and check. I really need that money.' 'This is the ROYAL Mail. Until it goes through the letterbox it's the property of Her Majesty The Queen. Can't let people take it willy-nilly. Now get back to work and put that letter on the belt.'

And so on. The envelope tsunamis kept coming. Tens of thousands of letters each night. Scores of thousands. Every night.

I'd read some of Bukowski's work before circumstances drove me to the job in the sorting office, and the film *Barfly* had just come out, starring Mickey Rourke and Faye Dunaway, based on Bukowski's early life as a bum, so I had some idea of who he was and what he was about. I'd read the novel *Women*, and a couple of his poetry collections had been my sole companions on many daytime drinking sprees. I'd liked what I'd read, but the only editions of his books available at that time were expensive American imports, so his was one of the names I'd look out for on the cheap second-hand bookstalls in the market square. Which was where I found *Post Office*, in a nice hardback, fine condition, two quid. I could barely afford even that meagre amount; most of my earnings were being given up to debtors, so that I wouldn't be evicted from my bedsit or taken to court or have my legs broken, and anything left over went on food and drink. I couldn't afford to buy books. And I didn't want to half-inch this one because I knew and liked the stall-holder, so I handed over the two quid and prepared myself to go hungry for a day. Maybe I could scrounge a few spuds from the couple upstairs, or a tin of soup from the feller below. Steal from the communal fridge. Something.

Food quickly ceased to matter. I took the book home, sat in my chair by the window, and, in the few hours I had to myself before I had to clock on at the sorting office, read the entire thing twice. I devoured it . . . the cool messiness of the writing and how it managed somehow to imbue mundane ritual with a mythological weight; how it helped me to feel that what I was doing, what I was being forced to do in order to continue breathing, were scenes in a life lived specially; the validity of the individual experience gulped in a vast and featureless organisation (the mail was Royal, I was never allowed to forget, it belonged to The Queen). I knew, reading it, that the tedium of that night's work to come would be just a little bit more bearable. The book tosses you about like a choppy sea; you're laughing, then you're feeling the heartbreak of the narrator's return to Betty, and then his anguished rage at her premature death, and then you're immersed in Bukowski's metaphor for existence – horseracing – and then you're back to laughing. The book throws you about all over the place. In truth, the post office features rarely, at least in any immediate sense, although it looms like a war in the background, behind the stuff about relationships and writing and the fun and frozen wastes of being alive.

And, of course, there's more to it than that. Central to much of Bukowski's work is a striving towards a kind of Zen-like detachment, a reaching of the perennial Outsider towards some understanding of his place in a world which he feels to be botched (*Post Office*'s opening line – 'It began as a mistake' – resonates in this respect), and to seek the meaning, if there is one to be sought, in his capacity and role as alien. America, or the stage of human evolution that post-war America represents, has jettisoned its soul; the clock is dominant, technology is choking, the manufactured and accepted need to consume has replaced any hunger for spiritual sustenance. And in the underground figure are battles for the fulfilment of base needs and the demand to live a worthwhile existence, through sex and love and laughter and booze and music and the written word. Bukowski was writing about Los Angeles; I was working in a sorting office on the outskirts of Cambridge. But I knew exactly what he was talking about. 'Mailman, you got any mail for me?' his postman-narrator is asked, and he screams in reply: 'Lady, how the hell do I know who you are or I am or anybody is?' We're forced into absurd lives, against which the only sane response is to wage a guerrilla operation of humour and lust and madness. The post office, or any world of work, is only one institutionalised system of control that is designed to beat people, to condition them into accepting that humiliation and failure is the norm. Those who do not rebel against this lose any ability to think for themselves. The workers are robbed of power whilst the bosses have only a small amount of it and can only use it arbitrarily, which is to say, pointlessly. In *Post Office* this situation is seen not only in the titular establishment but also in human interactions, marriage, consumerism, the hippy movement. Far from being hopeless, though, or despairing, we're shown that in resisting lies the potential for growth. These arenas – which are encapsulated in the phrase 'war all the time', as the title of one of Bukowski's many poetry collections has it – with their intricate systems of power and control, offer, in fact, an environment in which the human animal, in all its wildness, can flourish.

So the influence of Bukowski is more attitudinal than literary or stylistic. His novels – and *Post Office*, being his first, is no exception – are messy, ramshackle, rambling, structurally chaotic, held together, it seems, by bits of Sellotape and string. Even the punctuation defies basic grammatical rules. Yet to criticise it with the exegetical tools of formal literary appreciation is to entirely miss the point; the disorder of it, the near illiteracy of it, even, is of a piece with the explicit command it contains to construct a uniquely personal set of rules and beliefs as a way of resisting absorption and remaining, in a very real sense of the word, alive. This was vital to me at the time, living as I was surrounded by ivied halls and towers in which literature was unstintingly drained of all blood and relevance. It remains so. Bukowski's work, with less mess, with less chaos, with more reins and restrictions, would lose most of its value and charm.

He was an astonishingly prolific writer, Bukowski, producing scores of volumes of letters and poetry and essays and short stories and novels and screenplays and journals, some of it great, some of it good, some of it bad, some of it terrible. But the work thrusts itself into the world as he did himself; beer-bellied, flatulent, crude, aggressive, sensitive, acne-scarred, everything. It must be taken as a whole. When that envelope was eventually put through my letterbox it contained not the cheque I was praying for but a final threat of eviction; I was able to laugh, and sign up for more overtime at the sorting office, feeling less pain than I would've done before I read the book you're holding in your hands right now. And if this is your first contact with this odd and unique writer's work, and you want to read more, then be happy because there's a huge wave of it out there. Ah yip.

## CODE OF ETHICS

The attention of all employees is directed to the Code of Ethics for postal employees as set forth in Part 742 of the Postal Manual, and Conduct of Employees as outlined in Part 744 of the Postal Manual.

Postal employees have, over the years, established a fine tradition of faithful service to the Nation, unsurpassed by other groups. Each employee should take great pride in this tradition of dedicated service. Each of us must strive to make his contribution worthwhile in the continued movement of the Postal Service toward future progress in the public interest.

All postal personnel must act with unwavering integrity and complete devotion to the public interest. Postal personnel are expected to maintain the highest moral principles, and to uphold the laws of the United States and the regulations and policies of the Post Office Department. Not only is ethical conduct required, but officials and employees must be alert to avoid actions which would appear to prevent fulfillment of postal obligations. Assigned duties must be discharged conscientiously and effectively. The Postal Service has the unique privilege of having daily contact with the majority of the citizens of the Nation, and is, in many instances, their most direct contact with the Federal Government. Thus, there is an especial opportunity and responsibility for each postal employee to act with honor and integrity worthy of the public trust;

thereby reflecting credit and distinction on the Postal Service and on the entire Federal Government.

All employees are requested to review Part 742, Postal Manual, Basic Standards of Ethical Conduct, Personal Behavior of Employees, Restrictions on Political Activity, etc.

Officer in Charge

*This is presented as a work of fiction
and dedicated to nobody*

# I

## 1

IT BEGAN AS a mistake.

It was Christmas season and I learned from the drunk up the hill, who did the trick every Christmas, that they would hire damned near anybody, and so I went and the next thing I knew I had this leather sack on my back and was hiking around at my leisure. What a job, I thought. Soft! They only gave you a block or 2 and if you managed to finish, the regular carrier would give you another block to carry, or maybe you'd go back in and the soup would give you another, but you just took your time and shoved those Xmas cards in the slots.

I think it was my second day as a Christmas temp that this big woman came out and walked around with me as I delivered letters. What I mean by big was that her ass was big and her tits were big and that she was big in all the right places. She seemed a bit crazy but I kept looking at her body and I didn't care.

She talked and talked and talked. Then it came out. Her husband was an officer on an island far away and she got lonely, you know, and lived in this little house in back all by herself.

"What little house?" I asked.

She wrote the address on a piece of paper.

"I'm lonely too," I said, "I'll come by and we'll talk tonight."

I was shacked but the shackjob was gone half the time, off somewhere, and I was lonely all right. I was lonely for that big ass standing beside me.

"All right," she said, "see you tonight."

She was a good one all right, she was a good lay but like all lays after the 3rd or 4th night I began to lose interest and didn't go back.

But I couldn't help thinking, god, all these mailmen do is drop in their letters and get laid. This is the job for me, oh yes yes yes.

# 2

SO I TOOK the exam, passed it, took the physical, passed it, and there I was—a substitute mail carrier. It began easy. I was sent to West Avon Station and it was just like Christmas except I didn't get laid. Every day I expected to get laid but I didn't. But the soup was easy and I strolled around doing a block here and there. I didn't even have a uniform, just a cap. I wore my regular clothes. The way my shackjob Betty and I drank there was hardly money for clothes.

Then I was transferred to Oakford Station.

The soup was a bullneck named Jonstone. Help was needed there and I understood why. Jonstone liked to wear dark-red shirts—that meant danger and blood. There were 7 subs—Tom Moto, Nick Pelligrini, Herman Stratford, Rosey Anderson, Bobby Hansen, Harold Wiley and me, Henry Chinaski. Reporting time was 5 a.m. and I was the only drunk there. I always drank until past midnight, and there we'd sit, at 5 a.m. in the morning, waiting to get on the clock, waiting for some regular to call in sick. The regulars usually called in sick when it rained or during a heatwave or the day after a holiday when the mail load was doubled.

There were 40 or 50 different routes, maybe more, each case was different, you were never able to learn any of them, you had to get your mail up and ready before 8 a.m. for the truck dispatches, and Jonstone would take no excuses. The subs routed their magazines on corners, went without lunch, and died in the streets. Jonstone would have us start casing the routes 30 minutes late—spinning in his chair in his red shirt—"Chinaski take route 539!" We'd start a halfhour short but were still expected to get the mail up and out and be back on time. And once or twice a week, already beaten, fagged and fucked we had to make the night pickups, and the schedule on the board was impossible—the truck wouldn't go that fast. You had to skip four or five boxes on the first run and the next time around they were stacked with mail and you stank, you ran with sweat jamming it into the sacks. I got laid all right. Jonstone saw to that.

# 3

THE SUBS THEMSELVES made Jonstone possible by obeying his impossible orders. I couldn't see how a man of such obvious cruelty could be allowed to have his position. The regulars didn't care, the union man was worthless, so I filled out a thirty page report on one of my days off, mailed one copy to Jonstone and took the other down to the Federal Building. The clerk told me to wait. I waited and waited and waited. I waited an hour and thirty minutes, then was taken in to see a little grey-haired man with eyes like cigarette ash. He didn't even ask me to sit down. He began screaming at me as I entered the door.

"You're a wise son of a bitch, aren't you?"

"I'd rather you didn't curse me, sir!"

"Wise son of a bitch, you're one of those sons of bitches with a vocabulary and you like to lay it around!"

He waved my papers at me. And screamed: "MR. JONSTONE IS A FINE MAN!"

"Don't be silly. He's an obvious sadist," I said.

"How long have you been in the Post Office?"

"3 weeks."

"MR. JONSTONE HAS BEEN WITH THE POST OFFICE FOR 30 YEARS!"

"What does *that* have to do with it?"

"I said, MR. JONSTONE IS A FINE MAN!"

I believe the poor fellow actually wanted to kill me. He and Jonstone must have slept together.

"All right," I said, "Jonstone is a fine man. Forget the whole fucking thing." Then I walked out and took the next day off. Without pay, of course.

# 4

WHEN JONSTONE SAW me the next 5 a.m. he spun in his swivel and his face and his shirt were the same color. But he said nothing. I didn't care. I had been up to 2 a.m. drinking and screwing with Betty. I leaned back and closed my eyes.

At 7 a.m. Jonstone swiveled again. All the other subs had been assigned jobs or been sent to other stations that needed help.

"That's all, Chinaski. Nothing for you today."

He watched my face. Hell, I didn't care. All I wanted to do was to go to bed and get some sleep.

"O.K. Stone," I said. Among the carriers he was known as "The Stone," but I was the only one who addressed him that way.

I walked out, the old car started and soon I was back in bed with Betty.

"Oh, Hank! How nice!"

"Damn right, baby!" I pushed up against her warm tail and was asleep in 45 seconds.

# 5

BUT THE NEXT morning it was the same thing:

"That's all, Chinaski. Nothing for you today."

It went on for a week. I sat there each morning from 5 a.m. to 7 a.m. and didn't get paid. My name was even taken off the night collection run.

Then Bobby Hansen, one of the older subs—in length of service—told me, "He did that to me once. He tried to starve me."

"I don't care. I'm not kissing his ass. I'll quit or starve, anything."

"You don't have to. Report to Prell Station each night. Tell the soup you aren't getting any work and you can sit in as a special delivery sub."

"I can do that? No rules against it?"

"I got a paycheck every two weeks."

"Thanks, Bobby."

# 6

I FORGET THE beginning time. 6 or 7 p.m. Something like that.

All you did was sit with a handful of letters, take a streetmap and figure your run. It was easy. All the drivers took much more time than was needed to figure their runs and I played right along with them. I left when everybody left and came back when everybody came back.

Then you made another run. There was time to sit around in coffeeshops, read newspapers, feel decent. You even had time for lunch. Whenever I wanted a day off, I took one. On one of the routes there was this big young gal who got a special every night. She was a manufacturer of sexy dresses and nightgowns and *wore* them. You'd run up her steep stairway about 11 p.m., ring the bell and give her the special. She'd let out a bit of a gasp, like, "OOOOOOOOOOOOOOOOOhhhhhhhhhHHHH!", and she'd stand close, very, and she wouldn't let you leave while she read it, and then she'd say, "OOOOOOOOOh, goodnight, thank YOU!"

"Yes, mam," you'd say, trotting off with a dick like a bull's.

But it was not to last. It came in the mail after about a week and a half of freedom.

"Dear Mr. Chinaski:
You are to report to Oakford Station immediately. Refusal to do so will result in possible disciplinary action or dismissal.
A.E. Jonstone, Supt., Oakford Station."

I was back on the cross again.

# 7

"CHINASKI! TAKE ROUTE 539!"
The toughest in the station. Apartment houses with boxes that had scrubbed-out names or no names at all,

under tiny lightbulbs in dark halls. Old ladies standing in halls, up and down the streets, asking the same question as if they were one person with one voice:

"Mailman, you got any mail for me?"

And you felt like screaming "Lady, how the *hell* do I know who *you* are or I am or anybody is?"

The sweat dripping, the hangover, the impossibility of the schedule, and Jonstone back there in his red shirt, knowing it, enjoying it, pretending he was doing it to keep costs down. But everybody knew why he was doing it. Oh, what a fine man he was!

The people. The people. And the dogs.

Let me tell you about the dogs. It was one of those 100 degree days and I was running along, sweating, sick, delirious, hung-over. I stopped at a small apartment house with the box downstairs along the front pavement. I popped it open with my key. There wasn't a sound. Then I felt something jamming its way into my crotch. It moved way up there, I looked around and there was a German Shepherd, full-grown, with his nose halfway up my ass. With one snap of his jaws he could rip off my balls. I decided that those people were not going to get their mail that day, and maybe never get any mail again. Man, I mean he worked that nose in there. SNUFF! SNUFF! SNUFF!

I put the mail back into the leather pouch, and then very slowly, very, I took a half step forward. The nose followed. I took another half step with the other foot. The nose followed. Then I took a slow, very slow full step. Then another. Then stood still. The nose was out. And he just stood there looking at me. Maybe he'd never smelled anything like it and didn't quite know what to do.

I walked quietly away.

# 8

THERE WAS ANOTHER German Shepherd. It was hot summer and he came BOUNDING out of a back yard and then LEAPED through the air. His teeth snapped, just missing my jugular vein.

"OH JESUS!" I hollered, "OH JESUS CHRIST! MURDER! MURDER! HELP! MURDER!"

The beast turned and leaped again. I socked his head good in mid-air with the mail sack, letters and magazines flying out. He was ready to leap again when two guys, the owners, came out and grabbed him. Then, as he watched and growled, I reached down and picked up the letters and magazines that I would have to re-route on the front porch of the next house.

"You sons of bitches are crazy," I told the two guys, "that dog's a killer. Get rid of him or keep him off the street!"

I would have fought them both but there was that dog growling and lunging between them. I went over to the next porch and re-routed my mail on hands and knees.

As usual, I didn't have time for lunch, but I was still forty minutes late getting in.

The Stone looked at his watch. "You're 40 minutes late."

"You never arrived," I told him.

"That's a write-up."

"Sure it is, Stone."

He already had the proper form in the typer and was at it. As I sat casing up the mail and doing the go-backs he walked up and threw the form in front of me. I was tired of reading his write-ups and knew from my trip downtown that any protest was useless. Without looking I threw it into the wastebasket.

# 9

EVERY ROUTE HAD its traps and only the regular carriers knew of them. Each day it was another god damned thing, and you were always ready for a rape, murder, dogs, or insanity of some sort. The regulars wouldn't tell you their little secrets. That was the only advantage they had— except knowing their case by heart. It was gung ho for a new man, especially one who drank all night, went to bed at 2 a.m., rose at 4:30 a.m. after screwing and singing all night long, and, almost, getting away with it.

One day I was out on the street and the route was going well, though it was a new one, and I thought, Jesus Christ, maybe for the first time in two years I'll be able to eat lunch.

I had a terrible hangover, but still all went well until I came to this handful of mail addressed to a church. The address had no street number, just the name of the church, and the boulevard it faced. I walked, hungover, up the steps. I couldn't find a mailbox in there and no people in there. Some candles burning. Little bowls to dip your fingers in. And the empty pulpit looking at me, and all the statues, pale red and blue and yellow, the transoms shut, a stinking hot morning.

Oh Jesus Christ, I thought.

And walked out.

I went around to the side of the church and found a stairway going down. I went in through an open door. Do you know what I saw? A row of toilets. And showers. But it was dark. All the lights went out. How in hell can they expect a man to find a mailbox in the dark? Then I saw the light switch. I threw the thing and the lights in the church went on, inside and out. I walked into the next room and there were priests' robes spread out on a table. There was a bottle of wine.

For Christ's sake, I thought, who in hell but me would ever get caught in a scene like this?

I picked up the bottle of wine, had a good drag, left the letters on the robes, and walked back to the showers and toilets. I turned off the lights and took a shit in the dark and smoked a cigarette. I thought about taking a shower but I could see the headlines: MAILMAN CAUGHT DRINKING THE BLOOD OF GOD AND TAKING A SHOWER, NAKED, IN ROMAN CATHOLIC CHURCH.

So, finally, I didn't have time for lunch and when I got in Jonstone wrote me off for being twenty-three minutes off schedule.

I found out later that mail for the church was delivered to the parish house around the corner. But now, of course, I'll know where to shit and shower when I'm down and out.

## 10

THE RAINY SEASON began. Most of the money went for drink so my shoes had holes in the soles and my raincoat was torn and old. In any steady downpour I got quite wet, and I mean wet down to soaked and soggy shorts and stockings. The regular carriers called in sick, they called in sick from stations all over the city, so there was work everyday at Oakford Station, at all the stations. Even the subs were calling in sick. I didn't call in sick because I was too tired to think properly. This particular morning I was sent to Wently Station. It was one of those 5 day storms where the rain comes down in one continuous wall of water and the whole city gives up, everything gives up, the sewers can't swallow the water fast enough, the water comes up over the curbings, and in some sections, up on the lawn and into the houses.

I was sent off to Wently Station.

"They said they need a good man," the Stone called after me as I stepped out into a sheet of water.

The door closed. If the old car started, and it did, I was off to Wently. But it didn't matter—if the car didn't run, they threw you on a bus. My feet were already wet.

The Wently soup stood me in front of this case. It was already stuffed and I began stuffing more mail in with the help of another sub. I'd never seen such a case! It was a rotten joke of some sort. I counted 12 tie-outs on the case. That case must have covered half the city. I had yet to learn that the route was all steep hills. Whoever had conceived it was a madman.

We got it up and out and just as I was about to leave the soup walked over and said, "I can't give you any help on this."

"That's all right," I said.

All right, hell. It wasn't until later that I found out he was Jonstone's best buddy.

The route started at the station. The first of twelve swings. I stepped into a sheet of water and worked my way downhill. It was the poor part of town—small houses and courts with mailboxes full of spiders, mailboxes hanging by one nail, old women inside rolling cigarettes and chewing tobacco and humming to their canaries and watching you, an idiot lost in the rain.

When your shorts get wet they slip down, down down they slip, down around the cheeks of your ass, a wet rim of a thing held up by the crotch of your pants. The rain ran the ink on some of the letters; a cigarette wouldn't stay lit. You had to keep reaching into the pouch for magazines. It was the first swing and I was already tired. My shoes were caked with mud and felt like boots. Every now and then I'd hit a slippery spot and almost go down.

A door opened and an old woman asked the question heard a hundred times a day:

"Where's the *regular* man, today?"

"Lady, PLEASE, how would *I* know? How in the hell would I know? I'm here and he's someplace else?"

"Oh, you *are* a *gooney* fellow!"

"A gooney fellow?"

"Yes."

I laughed and put a fat water-soaked letter in her hand, then went on to the next. Maybe uphill will be better, I thought.

Another Old Nelly, meaning to be nice, asked me, "Wouldn't you like to come in and have a cup of tea and dry off?"

"Lady, don't you realize we don't even have time to pull up our shorts?"

"Pull up your shorts?"

"YES, PULL UP OUR SHORTS!" I screamed at her and walked off into the wall of water.

I finished the first swing. It took about an hour. Eleven more swings, that's eleven more hours. Impossible, I thought. They must have hung the roughest one on me first.

Uphill was worse because you had to pull your own weight.

Noon came and went. Without lunch. I was on the 4th or 5th swing. Even on a dry day the route would have been impossible. This way it was so impossible you couldn't even think about it.

Finally I was so wet I thought I was drowning. I found a front porch that only leaked a little and stood there and managed to light a cigarette. I had about 3 quiet puffs when I heard a little old lady's voice behind me:

"Mailman! Mailman!"

"Yes, mam?" I asked.

"YOUR MAIL IS GETTING WET!"

I looked down at my pouch and sure enough, I had left the leather flap open. A drop or two had fallen in from a hole in the porch roof.

I walked off. That does it, I thought, only an idiot would go through what I am going through. I am going to find a telephone and tell them to come get their mail and jam their job. Jonstone wins.

The moment I decided to quit, I felt much better. Through the rain I saw a building at the bottom of the hill that looked like it might have a telephone in it. I was halfway up the hill. When I got down I saw it was a small cafe. There was a heater going. Well, shit, I thought, I might as well get dry. I took off my raincoat and my cap, threw the mailpouch on the floor and ordered a cup of coffee.

It was very black coffee. Remade from old coffee-grounds. The worst coffee I had ever tasted, but it was hot. I drank 3 cups and sat there an hour, until I was completely dry. Then I looked out: it had stopped raining! I went out and walked up the hill and began delivering mail again. I took my time and finished the route. On the 12th swing I was walking in twilight. By the time I returned to the station it was night.

The carrier's entrance was locked.

I beat on the tin door.

A little warm clerk appeared and opened the door.

"What the hell took you so long?" he screamed at me.

I walked over to the case and threw down the wet pouch full of go-backs, miscased mail and pickup mail. Then I took off my key and flipped it against the case. You were supposed to sign in and out for your key. I didn't bother. He was standing there.

13

I looked at him.

"Kid, if you say one more word to me, if you so much as sneeze, so help me God, I am going to kill you!"

The kid didn't say anything. I punched out.

The next morning I kept waiting for Jonstone to turn and say something. He acted as if nothing had happened. The rain stopped and all the regulars were no longer sick. The Stone sent 3 subs home without pay, one of them me. I almost loved him then.

I went on in and got up against Betty's warm ass.

# 11

BUT THEN IT began raining again. The Stone had me out on a thing called Sunday Collection, and if you're thinking of church, forget it. You picked up a truck at West Garage and a clipboard. The clipboard told you what streets, what time you were to be there, and how to get to the next pickup box. Like 2:32 p.m., Beecher and Avalon, L3 R2 (which meant left three blocks, right two) 2:35 p.m., and you wondered how you could pick up one box, then drive 5 blocks in 3 minutes and be finished cleaning out another box. Sometimes it took you over 3 minutes to clean out a Sunday box. And the boards weren't accurate. Sometimes they counted an alley as a street and sometimes they counted a street as an alley. You never knew where you were.

It was one of those continuous rains, not hard, but it *never* stopped. The territory I was driving was new to me but at least it was light enough to read the clipboard. But as it got darker it was harder to read (by the dashboard light) or locate the pickup boxes. Also the water was rising in the streets, and several times I had stepped into water up to my ankles.

Then the dashboard light went out. I couldn't read the clipboard. I had no idea where I was. Without the clipboard I was like a man lost in the desert. But the luck wasn't all bad—yet. I had two boxes of matches and before I made for each new pickup box, I would light a match, memorize the directions and drive on. For once, I had outwitted Adversity, that Jonstone up there in the sky, looking down, watching me.

Then I took a corner, leaped out to unload the box and when I got back the clipboard was GONE!

Jonstone in the Sky, have Mercy! I was lost in the dark and the rain. *Was* I some kind of idiot, actually? Did I make things happen to myself? It was possible. It was possible that I was subnormal, that I was lucky just to be alive.

The clipboard had been wired to the dashboard. I figured it must have flown out of the truck on the last sharp turn. I got out of the truck with my pants rolled up around my knees and started wading through a foot of water. It was dark. I'd never find the god damned thing! I walked along, lighting matches—but nothing, nothing. It had floated away. As I reached the corner I had sense enough to notice which way the current was moving and follow it. I saw an object floating along, lit a match, and there it WAS! The clipboard. *Impossible!* I could have kissed the thing. I waded back to the truck, got in, rolled my pantlegs down and really *wired* that board to the dash. Of course, I was way behind schedule by then but at least I'd found their dirty clipboard. I wasn't lost in the backstreets of Nowhere. I wouldn't have to ring a doorbell and ask somebody the way back to the post office garage.

I could hear some fucker snarling from his warm front-room:

"Well, well. You're a post office employee, *aren't* you? Don't you know the way back to your own garage?"

So I drove along, lighting matches, leaping into whirl-pools of water and emptying collection boxes. I was tired and wet and hungover, but I was usually that way and I waded through the weariness like I did the water. I kept thinking of a hot bath, Betty's fine legs, and—something to keep me going—a picture of myself in an easychair, drink in hand, the dog walking up, me patting his head.

But that was a long way off. The stops on the clipboard seemed endless and when I reached the bottom it said "Over" and I flipped the board and sure enough, there on the backside was *another* list of stops.

With the last match I made the last stop, deposited my mail at the station indicated, and it was a *load*, and then drove back toward the West Garage. It was in the west end of town and in the west the land was very flat, the drainage system couldn't handle the water and anytime it rained any length of time at all, they had what was called a "flood." The description was accurate.

Driving on in, the water rose higher and higher. I noticed stalled and abandoned cars all around. Too bad. All I wanted was to get in that chair with that glass of scotch in my hand and watch Betty's ass wobble around the room. Then at a signal I met Tom Moto, one of the other Jonstone subs.

"Which way you going in?" Moto asked.

"The shortest distance between 2 points, I was taught, is a straight line," I answered him.

"You better not," he told me. "I know that area. It's an ocean through there."

"Bullshit," I said, "all it takes is a little guts. Got a match?"

I lit up and left him at the signal.

Betty, baby, I'm coming!

Yeah.

The water got higher and higher but mail trucks are built high off the ground. I took the shortcut through the residential neighborhood, full speed, and water flew up all around me. It continued to rain, hard. There weren't any cars around. I was the only moving object.

Betty baby. Yeah.

Some guy standing on his front porch laughed at me and yelled, "THE MAIL MUST GO THROUGH!"

I cursed him and gave him the finger.

I noticed that the water was rising above the floorboards, whirling around my shoes, but I kept driving. Only 3 blocks to go!

Then the truck stopped.

Oh. Oh. Shit.

I sat there and tried to kick it over. It started once, then stalled. Then it wouldn't respond. I sat there looking at the water. It must have been 2 feet deep. What was I supposed to do? Sit there until they sent a rescue squad?

What did the Postal Manual say? Where was it? I had never known anybody who had seen one.

Balls.

I locked the truck, put the ignition keys in my pocket and stepped into the water—nearly up to my waist—and began wading toward West Garage. It was still raining. Suddenly the water rose another 3 or 4 inches. I had been walking across a lawn and had stepped off the curbing. The truck was parked on somebody's front lawn.

For a moment I thought that swimming might be faster, then I thought, no, that would look ridiculous. I made it to the garage and walked up to the dispatcher. There I was, wet as wet could get and he looked at me.

I threw him the truck keys and the ignition keys.

Then I wrote on a piece of paper: 3435 Mountview Place.

"Your truck's at this address. Go get it."

"You mean you left it out there?"

"I mean I left it out there."

I walked over, punched out, then stripped to my shorts and stood in front of a heater. I hung my clothes over the heater. Then I looked across the room and there by another heater stood Tom Moto in *his* shorts.

We both laughed.

"It's hell, isn't it?" he asked.

"Unbelievable."

"Do you think The Stone planned it?"

"Hell yes! He even made it rain!"

"Did you get stalled out there?"

"Sure," I said.

"I did too."

"Listen, baby," I said, "my car is 12 years old. You've got a new one. I'm sure I'm stalled out there. How about a push to get me started?"

"O.K."

We got dressed and went out. Moto had bought a new model car about 3 weeks before. I waited for his engine to start. Not a sound. Oh Christ, I thought.

The rain was up to the floorboards.

Moto got out.

"No good. It's dead."

I tried mine without any hope. There was some action from the battery, some spark, though feeble. I pumped for gas, hit it again. It started up. I really let it roar. VICTORY! I warmed it good. Then I backed up and began to push Moto's new car. I pushed him for a mile. The thing wouldn't even fart. I pushed him into a garage, left him there, and picking the highland and the drier streets, made it back to Betty's ass.

# 12

THE STONE'S FAVORITE carrier was Matthew Battles. Battles never came in with a wrinkled shirt on. In fact, everything he wore was new, looked new. The shoes, the shirts, the pants, the cap. His shoes really shined and none of his clothing appeared to have ever been laundered even once. Once a shirt or a pair of pants became the least bit soiled he threw them away.

The Stone often said to us as Matthew walked by:

"Now, *there* goes a carrier!"

And The Stone meant it. His eyes damn near shimmered with love.

And Matthew would stand at his case, erect and clean, scrubbed and well-slept, shoes gleaming victoriously, and he would fan those letters into the case with joy.

"You're a real carrier, Matthew!"

"Thank you, Mr. Jonstone!"

ONE 5 A.M. I walked in and sat down to wait behind The Stone. He looked a bit slumped under that red shirt.

Moto was next to me. He told me: "They picked up Matthew yesterday."

"Picked him up?"

"Yeah, for stealing from the mails. He'd been opening letters for the Nekalayla Temple and taking money out. After 15 years on the job."

"How'd they get him, how'd they find out?"

"The old ladies. The old ladies had been sending in letters to Nekalayla filled with money and they weren't getting any thankyou notes or response. Nekalayla told the P.O. and the P.O. put the Eye on Matthew. They found him opening letters down at the soak-box, taking money out."

"No shit?"

"No shit. They caught him in cold daylight."

I leaned back.

Nekalayla had built this large temple and painted it a sickening green, I guess it reminded him of money, and he had an office staff of 30 or 40 people who did nothing but open envelopes, take out checks and money, record the amount, the sender, date received and so on. Others were busy mailing out books and pamphlets written by Nekalayla, and his photo was on the wall, a large one of N. in priestly robes and beard, and a painting of N., very large too, looked over the office, watching.

Nekalayla claimed he had once been walking through the desert when he met Jesus Christ and Jesus Christ told him everything. They sat on a rock together and J.C. laid it on him. Now he was passing the secrets on to those who could afford it. He also held a service every Sunday. His help, who were also his followers, rang in and out on timeclocks.

Imagine Matthew Battles trying to outwit Nekalayla who had met Christ in the desert!

"Has anybody said anything to The Stone?" I asked.

"Are you *kidding?*"

We sat an hour or so. A sub was assigned to Matthew's case. The other subs were given other jobs. I sat alone behind The Stone. Then I got up and walked to his desk.

"Mr. Jonstone?"

"Yes, Chinaski?"

"Where's Matthew today? Sick?"

The Stone's head dropped. He looked at the paper in his hand and pretended to continue reading it. I walked back and sat down.

At 7 a.m. The Stone turned:

"There's nothing for you today, Chinaski."

I stood up and walked to the doorway. I stood in the doorway. "Good morning, Mr. Jonstone. Have a good day."

He didn't answer. I walked down to the liquor store and bought a half pint of Grandad for my breakfast.

# 13

THE VOICES OF the people were the same, no matter where you carried the mail you heard the same things over and over again.

"You're late, aren't you?"

"Where's the regular carrier?"

"Hello, Uncle Sam!"

"Mailman! Mailman! This doesn't go here!"

The streets were full of insane and dull people. Most of them lived in nice houses and didn't seem to work, and you wondered how they did it. There was one guy who wouldn't let you put the mail in his box. He'd stand in the driveway and watch you coming for 2 or 3 blocks and he'd stand there and hold his hand out.

I asked some of the other guys who had carried the route:

"What's wrong with that guy who stands and holds his hand out?"

"What guy who stands there and holds his hand out?" they asked.

They all had the same voice too.

One day when I had the route, the man-who-holds-his-hand-out was a half a block up the street. He was talking to a neighbor, looked back at me more than a block away and knew he had time to walk back and meet me. When he turned his back to me, I began running. I don't believe

I ever delivered mail that fast, all stride and motion, never stopping or pausing, I was going to kill him. I had the letter half in the slot of his box when he turned and saw me.

"OH NO NO NO!" he screamed, "DON'T PUT IT IN THE BOX!"

He ran down the street toward me. All I saw was the blur of his feet. He must have run a hundred yards in 9.2.

I put the letter in his hand. I watched him open it, walk across the porch, open the door and go into his house. What it meant somebody else will have to tell me.

# 14

AGAIN I WAS on a new route. The Stone always put me on hard routes, but now. and then, due to the circumstances of things, he was forced to place me on one less murderous. Route 511 was peeling off quite nicely, and there I was thinking about *lunch* again, the lunch that never came.

It was an average residential neighborhood. No apartment houses. Just house after house with well-kept lawns. But it was a *new* route and I walked along wondering where the trap was. Even the weather was nice.

By god, I thought, I'm going to make it! Lunch, and back in on schedule! Life, at last, was bearable.

These people didn't even own dogs. Nobody stood outside waiting for their mail. I hadn't heard a human voice in hours. Perhaps I had reached my postal maturity, whatever that was. I strolled along, efficient, almost dedicated.

I remembered one of the older carriers pointing to his heart and telling me, "Chinaski, someday it will get you, it will get you right *here!*"

"Heart attack?"

"Dedication to service. You'll see. You'll be proud of it."

"Balls!"

But the man had been sincere.

I thought about him as I walked along.

Then I had a registered letter with return attached.

I walked up and rang the doorbell. A little window opened in the door. I couldn't see the face.

"Registered letter!"

"Stand back!" said a woman's voice. "Stand back so I can see your face!"

Well, there it was, I thought, another nut.

"Look lady, you don't *have* to see my face. I'll just leave this slip in the mailbox and you can pick your letter up at the station. Bring proper identification."

I put the slip in the mailbox and began to walk off the porch.

The door opened and she ran out. She had on one of those see-through negligees and no brassiere. Just dark blue panties. Her hair was uncombed and stuck out as if it were trying to run away from her. There seemed to be some type of cream on her face, most of it under her eyes. The skin on her body was white as if it never saw sunlight and her face had an unhealthy look. Her mouth hung open. She had on a touch of lipstick, and she was *built* all the way . . .

I caught all this as she rushed at me. I was sliding the registered letter back into the pouch.

She screamed, "Give me my letter!"

I said, "Lady, you'll have to . . ."

She grabbed the letter and ran to the door, opened it and ran in.

God damn! You couldn't come back without either the registered letter or a signature! You even had to sign in and out with the things.

23

"HEY!"

I went after her and jammed my foot into the door just in time.

"HEY, GOD DAMN YOU!"

"Go away! Go away! You are an evil man!"

"Look, lady! Try to understand! You've got to sign for that letter! I can't let you have it that way! You are robbing the United States mails!"

"Go away, evil man!"

I put all my weight against the door and pushed into the room. It was dark in there. All the shades were down. All the shades in the house were down.

"YOU HAVE NO RIGHT IN MY HOUSE! GET OUT!"

"And you have no right to rob the mails! Either give me the letter back or sign for it. Then I'll leave."

"All right! All right! I'll sign."

I showed her where to sign and gave her a pen. I looked at her breasts and the rest of her and I thought, what a shame she's crazy, what a shame, what a shame.

She handed back the pen and her signature—it was just scrawled. She opened the letter, began to read it as I turned to leave.

Then she was in front of the door, arms spread across. The letter was on the floor.

"Evil evil evil man! You came here to rape me!"

"Look lady, let me by."

"THERE IS EVIL WRITTEN ALL OVER YOUR FACE!"

"Don't you think I know that? Now let me out of here!"

With one hand I tried to push her aside. She clawed one side of my face, good. I dropped my bag, my cap fell off, and as I held a handkerchief to the blood she came up and raked the other side.

"YOU CUNT! WHAT THE HELL'S WRONG WITH YOU!"

"See there? See there? You're evil!"

She was right up against me. I grabbed her by the ass and got my mouth on hers. Those breasts were against me, she was all up against me. She pulled her head back, away from me—

"Rapist! Rapist! Evil rapist!"

I reached down with my mouth, got one of her tits, then switched to the other.

"Rape! Rape! I'm being raped!"

She was right. I got her pants down, unzipped my fly, got it in, then walked her backwards to the couch. We fell down on top of it.

She lifted her legs high.

"RAPE!" she screamed.

I finished her off, zipped my fly, picked up my mail pouch and walked out leaving her staring quietly at the ceiling . . .

I MISSED lunch but still couldn't make the schedule.

"You're 15 minutes late," said The Stone.

I didn't say anything.

The Stone looked at me. "God o mighty, what happened to your face?" he asked.

"What happened to yours?" I asked him.

"Whadda you mean?"

"Forget it."

# 15

I WAS HUNGOVER again, another heat spell was on—a week of 100 degree days. The drinking went on each night, and in the early mornings and days there was The Stone and the impossibility of everything.

Some of the boys wore African sun helmets and shades, but me, I was about the same, rain or shine—ragged clothing, and the shoes so old that the nails were always driving into my feet. I put pieces of cardboard in the shoes. But it only helped temporarily—soon the nails would be eating into my heels again.

The whiskey and beer ran out of me, fountained from the armpits, and I drove along with this load on my back like a cross, puffing out magazines, delivering thousands of letters, staggering, welded to the side of the sun.

Some woman screamed at me:

"MAILMAN! MAILMAN! THIS DOESN'T GO HERE!"

I looked. She was a block back down the hill and I was already behind schedule.

"Look, lady, put the letter outside your mailbox! We'll pick it up tomorrow!"

"NO! NO! I WANT YOU TO TAKE IT NOW!"

She waved the thing around in the sky.

"Lady!"

"COME GET IT! IT DOESN'T BELONG HERE!"

Oh my god.

I dropped the sack. Then I took my cap and threw it on the grass. It rolled out into the street. I left it and walked down toward the woman. One half block.

I walked down and snatched the thing from her hand, turned, walked back.

It was an advertisement! 4th class mail. Something about a 1/2 off clothing sale.

I picked my cap up out of the street, put it on my head. Put the sack back onto the left side of my spine, started out again. 100 degrees.

I walked past one house and a woman ran out after me.

"Mailman! Mailman! Don't you have a letter for me?"

"Lady, if I didn't put one in your box, that means you don't have any mail."

"But I know you have a letter for me!"

"What makes you say that?"

"Because my sister phoned and said she was going to write me."

"Lady, I don't have a letter for you."

"I know you have! I know you have! I know it's there!"

She started to reach for a handful of letters.

"DON'T TOUCH THE UNITED STATES MAILS, LADY! THERE'S NOTHING FOR YOU TODAY!"

I turned and walked off.

"I KNOW YOU HAVE MY LETTER!"

Another woman stood on her porch.

"You're late today."

"Yes, mam."

"Where's the regular man today?"

"He's dying of cancer."

"Dying of cancer? Harold is dying of cancer?"

"That's right," I said.

I handed her mail to her.

"BILLS! BILLS! BILLS!" she screamed. "IS THAT ALL YOU CAN BRING ME? THESE BILLS?"

"Yes, mam, that's all I can bring you."

I turned and walked on.

It wasn't my fault that they used telephones and gas and light and bought all their things on credit. Yet when I brought them their bills they screamed at me—as if *I* had asked them to have a phone installed, or a $350 t.v. set sent over with no money down.

The next stop was a small two storey dwelling, fairly new, with ten or twelve units. The lock box was in the

27

front, under a porch roof. At last, a bit of shade. I put the key in the box and opened it.

"HELLO UNCLE SAM! HOW ARE YOU TODAY?"

He was loud. I hadn't expected that man's voice behind me. He had *screamed* at me, and being hungover I was nervous. I jumped in shock. It was too much. I took the key out of the box and turned. All I could see was a screen door. Somebody was back in there. Air-conditioned and invisible.

"God damn you!" I said, "don't call me Uncle Sam! I'm *not* Uncle Sam!"

"Oh you're one of those *wise* guys, eh? For 2 cents I'd come out and whip your ass!"

I took my pouch and slammed it to the ground. Magazines and letters flew everywhere. I would have to reroute the whole swing. I took off my cap, and smashed it to the cement.

"COME OUT OF THERE, YOU SON OF A BITCH! OH, GOD O MIGHTY, I BEG YOU! COME OUT OF THERE! COME OUT, COME OUT OF THERE!"

I was ready to murder him.

Nobody came out. There wasn't a sound. I looked at the screen door. Nothing. It was as if the apartment were empty. For a moment I thought of going in. Then I turned, got down on my knees and began rerouting the letters and magazines. It's a job without a case. Twenty minutes later I had the mail up. I stuck some letters in the lock box, turned, looked at the screen door again. Still not a sound.

I finished the route, walking along, thinking, well, he'll phone and tell Jonstone that I threatened him. When I get in I better be ready for the worst.

I swung the door open and there was The Stone at his desk, reading something.

I stood there, looking down at him, waiting.

The Stone glanced up at me, then down at what he was reading.

I kept standing there, waiting.

The Stone kept reading.

"Well," I finally said, "what about it?"

"What about what?" The Stone looked up.

"ABOUT THE PHONE CALL! TELL ME ALL ABOUT THE PHONE CALL! DON'T JUST SIT THERE!"

"What phone call?"

"You didn't get a phone call about me?"

"A phone call? What happened? What have you been doing out there? What did you do?"

"Nothing."

I walked over and checked my stuff in.

The guy hadn't phoned in. No grace on his part. He probably thought I would come back if he phoned in.

I walked past The Stone on my way back to the case.

"What did you *do* out there, Chinaski?"

"Nothing."

My act so confused The Stone that he forgot to tell me I was 30 minutes late or write me up for it.

# 16

I was casing next to G.G. early one morning. That's what they called him: G.G. His actual name was George Greene. But for years he was simply called G.G. and after a while he looked like G.G. He had been a carrier since his early twenties and now he was in his late sixties. His voice was gone. He didn't speak. He croaked. And when he croaked, he didn't say much. He was neither liked nor disliked. He was just there. His face had wrinkled into strange runs and mounds of unattractive flesh. No light shone from his face. He was just a hard old crony who had done his job: G.G. The eyes looked like dull bits of clay dropped into the eye sockets. It was best if you didn't think about him or look at him.

But G.G., having all that seniority had one of the easiest routes, right out on the fringe of the rich district. In fact, you might call it the rich district. Although the houses were old, they were large, most of them two stories high. Wide lawns mowed and kept green by Japanese gardeners. Some movie stars lived there. A famous cartoonist. A best-selling writer. Two former governors. Nobody ever spoke to you in that area. You never saw anybody. The only time you saw anybody was at the beginning of the route where there were less expensive homes, and here the children bothered you. I mean, G.G. was a bachelor. And he had this whistle. At the beginning of his route, he'd stand tall and straight, take out the whistle, a large one, and blow it, spit flying out in all directions. That was to let the children know he was there. He had candy for the children. And they'd come running out and he'd give them candy as he went down the street. Good old G.G.

I'd found out about the candy the first time I got the route. The Stone didn't like to give me a route that easy but sometimes he couldn't help it. So I walked along and this young boy came out and asked me,

"Hey, where's my candy?"

And I said, "What candy, kid?"

And the kid said, "*My* candy! I want *my* candy!"

"Look, kid," I said, "you must be crazy. Does your mother just let you run around loose?"

The kid looked at me strangely.

BUT ONE day G.G. got into trouble. Good old G.G. He met this new little girl in the neighborhood. And gave her some candy. And said, "My, you're a *pretty* little girl! I'd like to have you for my own little girl!"

The mother had been listening at the window and she ran out screaming, accusing G.G. of child molestation. She hadn't known about G.G., so when she saw him give the girl candy and make that statement, it was too much for her.

Good old G.G. Accused of child molestation.

I came in and heard The Stone on the phone, trying to explain to the mother that G.G. was an honorable man. G.G. just sat in front of his case, transfixed.

When The Stone was finished and had hung up, I told him:

"You shouldn't suck up to that woman. She's got a dirty mind. Half the mothers in America, with their precious big pussies and their precious little daughters, half the mothers in America have dirty minds. Tell her to shove it. G.G. can't get his pecker hard, you know that."

The Stone shook his head. "No, the public's dynamite! They're dynamite!"

That's all he could say. I had seen The Stone before—posturing and begging and explaining to every nut who phoned in about anything . . .

I WAS CASING next to G.G. on route 501, which was not too bad, I had to fight to get the mail up but it was *possible*, and that gave one hope.

Although G.G. knew his case upsidedown, his hands were slowing. He had simply stuck too many letters in his life—even his sense-deafened body was finally revolting.

31

Several times during the morning I saw him falter. He'd stop and sway, go into a trance, then snap out of it and stick some more letters. I wasn't particularly fond of the man. His life hadn't been a brave one, and he had turned out to be a hunk of shit more or less. But each time he faltered, something tugged at me. It was just like a faithful horse who just couldn't go anymore. Or an old car, just giving it up one morning.

The mail was heavy and as I watched G.G. I got death-chills. For the first time in over 40 years he might miss the morning dispatch! For a man as proud of his job and his work as G.G., that could be a tragedy. I had missed plenty of morning dispatches, and had to take the sacks out to the boxes in my car, but my attitude was a bit different.

He faltered again.

God o mighty, I thought, doesn't anybody notice but me?

I looked around, nobody was concerned. They all professed, at one time or another, to be fond of him—"G.G.'s a good guy." But the "good old guy" was sinking and nobody cared. Finally I had less mail in front of me than G.G.

Maybe I can help him get his magazines up, I thought. But a clerk came along and dropped more mail in front of me and I was almost back with G.G. It was going to be close for both of us. I faltered for a moment, then clenched my teeth together, spread my legs, dug in like a guy who had just taken a hard punch, and winged the mass of letters in.

Two minutes before pull-down time, both G.G. and I had gotten our mail up, our mags routed and sacked, our airmail in. We were both going to make it. I had worried for nothing. Then The Stone came up. He carried two bundles of circulars. He gave one bundle to G.G. and the other to me.

"These must be worked in," he said, then walked off.

The Stone knew that we couldn't work those circs in and pull-down in time to meet the dispatch. I wearily cut the strings around the circs and started to case them in. G.G. just sat there and stared at his bundle of circs.

Then he put his head down, put his head down in his arms and began to cry softly.

I couldn't believe it.

I looked around.

The other carriers weren't looking, at G.G. They were pulling down their letters, strapping them out, talking and laughing with each other.

"Hey," I said a couple of times, "hey!"

But they wouldn't look at G.G.

I walked over to G.G. Touched him on the arm: "G.G.," I said, "what can I do for you?"

He jumped up from his case, ran up the stairway to the men's locker room. I watched him go. Nobody seemed to notice. I stuck a few more letters, then ran up the stairs myself.

There he was, head down in his arms on one of the tables. Only he wasn't quietly crying now. He was sobbing and wailing. His whole body shook in spasms. He wouldn't stop.

I ran down the steps, past all the carriers, and up to The Stone's desk.

"Hey, hey, Stone! Jesus Christ, Stone!"

"What is it?" he asked.

"G.G. has flipped out! Nobody cares! He's upstairs crying! He needs help!"

"Who's manning his route?"

"Who gives a damn? I tell you, he's *sick*! He needs help!"

"I gotta get somebody to man his route!"

The Stone got up from his desk, circled around looking at his carriers as if there might be an extra one somewhere. Then he hustled back to his desk.

"Look, Stone, somebody's got to take that man home. Tell me where he lives and I'll drive him home myself—off the clock. Then I'll carry your damned route."

The Stone looked up:

"Who's manning your case?"

"Oh, God damn the case!"

"GO MAN YOUR CASE!"

Then he was talking to another supervisor on the phone: "Hello, Eddie? Listen, I need a man out here . . ."

There'd be no candy for the kids that day. I walked back. All the other carriers were gone. I began sticking in the circulars. Over on G.G.'s case was his tie-up of unstuck circs. I was behind schedule again. Without a dispatch. When I came in late that afternoon, The Stone wrote me up.

I never saw G.G. again. Nobody knew what happened to him. Nor did anybody ever mention him again. The "good guy." The dedicated man. Knifed across the throat over a handful of circs from a local market with its special: a free box of a brand name laundry soap, with the coupon, and any purchase over $3.

# 17

AFTER 3 YEARS I made "regular." That meant holiday pay (subs didn't get paid for holidays) and a 40 hour week with 2 days off. The Stone was also forced to assign me as relief man to 5 different routes. That's all I had to carry—5 different routes. In time, I would learn the cases well plus the shortcuts and traps on each route. Each day would be easier. I could begin to cultivate that comfortable look.

Somehow, I was not too happy. I was not a man to deliberately seek pain, the job was still difficult enough, but somehow it lacked the old glamor of my sub days—the not-knowing-what-the-hell was going to happen next.

A few of the regulars came around and shook my hand. "Congratulations," they said.

"Yeh," I said.

Congratulations for what? I hadn't done anything. Now I was a member of the club. I was one of the boys. I could be there for years, eventually bid for my own route. Get Xmas presents from my people. And when I phoned in sick, they would say to some poor bastard sub, "Where's the *regular* man today? You're late. The regular man is never late."

So there I was. Then a bulletin came out that no caps or equipment were to be placed on top of the carrier's case. Most of the boys put their caps up there. It didn't hurt anything and saved a trip to the locker room. Now after 3 years of putting my cap up there I was ordered not to do so.

Well, I was still coming in hungover and I didn't have things like caps on my mind. So my cap was up there, the day after the order came out.

The Stone came running with his write-up. It said that it was against rules and regulations to have any equipment on top of the case. I put the write-up in my pocket and went on sticking letters. The Stone sat swiveled in his chair, watching me. All the other carriers had put their caps in their lockers. Except me and one other—one Marty. And The Stone had gone up to Marty and said, "Now, Marty, you read the order. Your cap isn't supposed to be on top of the case."

"Oh, I'm sorry, sir. Habit, you know. Sorry." Marty took his cap off the case and ran upstairs to his locker with it.

The next morning I forgot again. The Stone came with his write-up.

It said that it was against rules and regulations to have any equipment on top of the case.

I put the write-up in my pocket and went on sticking letters.

THE NEXT morning as I walked in, I could see The Stone watching me. He was very deliberate about watching me. He was waiting to see what I would do with the cap. I let him wait awhile. Then I took the cap off my head and placed it on top of the case.

The Stone ran up with his write-up.

I didn't read it. I threw it in the wastebasket, left my cap up there and went on sticking mail.

I could hear The Stone at his typewriter. There was anger in the sound of the keys.

I wondered how he managed to learn how to type? I thought.

He came again. Handed me a 2nd write-up.

I looked at him.

"I don't have. to read it. I know what it says. It says that I didn't read the first write-up."

I threw the 2nd write-up in the wastebasket.

The Stone ran back to his typewriter.

He handed me a 3rd write-up.

"Look," I said, "I know what all these things say. The first write-up was for having my cap on top of the case. The 2nd was for not reading the first. This 3rd one is for not reading the first or 2nd write-ups."

I looked at him, and then dropped the write-up into the wastebasket without reading it.

"Now I can throw these away as fast as you can type them. It can go on for hours, and soon one of us is going to begin looking ridiculous. It's up to you."

The Stone went back to his chair and sat down. He didn't type anymore. He just sat looking at me.

I DIDN'T go in the next day. I slept until noon. I didn't phone. Then I went down. to the Federal Building. I told them my mission. They put me in front of the desk of a thin old woman. Her hair was grey and she had a very thin neck that suddenly bent in the middle. It pushed her head forward and she looked up over the top of her glasses at me.

"Yes?"

"I want to resign."

"To *resign*?"

"Yes, resign."

"And you're a regular carrier?"

"Yes," I said.

"Tsk, tsk, tsk, tsk, tsk, tsk, tsk," she went, making this sound with her dry lips.

She gave me the proper papers and I sat there filling them out.

"How long have you been with the post office?"

"Three and one half years."

"Tsk, tsk, tsk, tsk, tsk, tsk, tsk, tsk," she went, "tsk, tsk, tsk, tsk."

And so there it was. I drove home to Betty and we uncapped the bottle.

Little did I know that in a couple of years I would be back as a clerk and that I would clerk, all hunched-up on a stool, for nearly 12 years.

# II

## 1

MEANWHILE, THINGS WENT on. I had a long run of luck at the racetrack. I began to feel confident out there. You went for a certain profit each day, somewhere between 15 and 40 bucks. You didn't ask too much. If you didn't hit early, you bet a little more, enough so that if the horse came in, you had your profit margin. I kept coming back, day after day, winners, giving Betty the thumb-up as I drove in the driveway.

Then Betty got a job as a typist, and when one of those shack-jobs gets a job, you notice the difference right away. We kept drinking each night and she left before I did in the morning, all hungover. Now she'd know what it was like. I got up around 10:30 a.m., had a leisurely cup of coffee and a couple of eggs, played with the dog, flirted with the young wife of a mechanic who lived in the back, got friendly with a stripteaser who lived in the front. I'd be at the track by one p.m., then back with my profit, and out with the dog at the bus stop to wait for Betty to come home. It was a good life.

Then, one night, Betty, my love, let me have it, over the first drink:

"Hank, I can't stand it!"

"You can't stand what, baby?"

"The situation."

"What situation, babe?"

"Me working and you laying around. All the neighbors think I am supporting you."

"Hell, I worked and *you* laid around."

"That's different. You're a man, I'm a woman."

"Oh, I didn't know that. I thought you bitches were always screaming for equal rights?"

"I know what's going on with little butterball in back, walking around in front of you with her tits hanging out . . ."

"Her *tits* hanging out?"

"Yes, her TITS! Those big white cow-tits!"

"Hmm . . . They are big at that."

"There! You see!"

"Now what the hell?"

"I've got friends around here. They see what's going on!"

"These aren't friends. Those are just mealy-mouthed gossips."

"And that whore up front who poses as a dancer."

"She's a whore?"

"She'll screw anything with a cock."

"You've gone crazy."

"I just don't want all these people thinking I am supporting you. All the neighbors . . ."

"God damn the neighbors! What do we care what they think? We never did before. Besides, *I'm* paying the rent. *I'm* buying the food! I'm making it at the track. Your money is yours. You never had it so good."

"No, Hank, it's over. I can't stand it!"

I got up and walked over to her.

"Now, come on baby, you're just a little upset tonight."

39

I tried to grab her. She pushed me away.

"All right, god damn it!" I said.

I walked back to my chair, finished my drink, had another.

"It's over," she said, "I'm not sleeping with you another night."

"All right. Keep your pussy. It's not that great."

"Do you want to keep the house or do you want to move out?" she asked.

"You keep the house."

"How about the dog?"

"You keep the dog," I said.

"He's going to miss you."

"I'm glad somebody is going to miss me."

I got up, walked to the car and I rented the first place I saw with a sign. I moved in that night.

I had just lost 3 women and a dog.

# 2

THE NEXT THING I knew, I had a young girl from Texas on my lap. I won't go into details of how I met her. Anyway, there it was. She was 23. I was 36.

She had long blonde hair and was good solid meat. I didn't know, at the time, that she also had plenty of money. She didn't drink but I did. We laughed a lot at first. And went to the racetrack together. She was a looker, and everytime I got back to my seat there would be some jerkoff sliding closer and closer to her. There were dozens of them. They just kept moving closer to her. Joyce would just sit. I had to handle them all one of two ways. Either take Joyce and move off or tell the guy:

"Look, buddy, this one's taken! Now move off!"

But fighting the wolves and the horses at the same time was too much for me. I kept losing. A pro goes to the track alone. I knew that. But I thought maybe I was exceptional. I found out that I wasn't exceptional at all. I could lose my money as fast as anybody.

Then Joyce demanded that we get married.

What the hell? I thought, I'm cooked anyhow.

I drove her to Vegas for a cheap wedding, then drove her right back.

I sold the car for ten dollars and the next thing I knew we were on a bus to Texas and when we landed I had 75 cents in my pocket. It was a very small town, the population, I believe, was under 2,000. The town had been picked by experts, in a national article, as the last town in the USA any enemy would attack with an atomic bomb. I could see why.

All this time, without knowing it, I was working my way back toward the post office. That mother.

Joyce had a little house in town and we laid around and screwed and ate. She fed me well, fattened me up and weakened me at the same time. She couldn't get enough. Joyce, my wife, was a nymph.

I took little walks through the town, alone, to get away from her, teethmarks all over my chest, neck and shoulders, and somewhere else that worried me more and was quite painful. She was eating me alive.

I limped through the town and they stared at me, knowing about Joyce, her sex drive, and also that her father and grandfather had more money, land, lakes, hunting preserves than all of them. They pitied and hated me at the same time.

A midget was sent to get me out of bed one morning and he drove me all over, pointing out this and that, Mr. so and so, Joyce's father owns that, and Mr. so and so, Joyce's grandfather owns that . . .

We drove all morning. Somebody was trying to scare me. I was bored. I sat in the back seat and the midget thought I was an operator, that I had worked my way into millions. He didn't know it was an accident, and that I was an ex-mail carrier with 75 cents in my pocket.

The midget, poor fellow, had a nervous disease and drove very fast, and every so often he'd shake all over and lose control of the car. It went from one side of the road to the other and once scraped along a fence for 100 yards before the midget got control of himself.

"HEY! EASY THERE, BUSTER!" I yelled at him from the back seat.

That was it. They were trying to knock me off. It was obvious. The midget was married to a very beautiful girl. When she was in her teens she got a coke bottle trapped in. her pussy and had to go to a doctor to get it out, and, like in all small towns, the word got around about the coke bottle, the poor girl was shunned, and the midget was the only taker. He'd ended up with the best piece of ass in town.

I lit up a cigar Joyce had given me and I told the midget, "That'll be all, buster. Now see that I get back. And drive slowly. I don't want to blow this game now."

I played the operator to please him.

"Yes, sir, Mr. Chinaski. Yes, sir!"

He admired me. He thought I was a son of a bitch.

When I got in, Joyce asked, "Well, did you see everything?"

"I saw enough," I said. Meaning, that they were trying to knock me off. I didn't know if Joyce was in on it or not.

Then she started peeling my clothes off and pushing me toward the bed.

"Now wait a minute, baby! We've already gone twice and it's not even 2 p.m. yet!"

She just giggled and kept on pushing.

# 3

HER FATHER REALLY hated me. He thought I was after his money. I didn't want his god damned money. And I didn't even want his god damned precious daughter.

The only time I ever saw him was when he walked into the bedroom one morning about 10 a.m. Joyce and I were in bed, resting up. Luckily we had just finished.

I peered at him from under the edge of the cover. Then I couldn't help myself. I smiled at him and gave him a big wink.

He ran out of the house growling and cursing.

If I could be removed, he'd certainly see to it.

Gramps was cooler. We'd go to his place and I'd drink whiskey with him and listen to his cowboy records. His old lady was simply indifferent. She neither liked or hated me. She fought with Joyce a lot and I sided with the old lady once or twice. That kind of won her over. But gramps was cool. I think he was in on the conspiracy.

We had been at this cafe and eaten, with everybody fawning over us and staring. There was gramps, grandma, Joyce, and I.

Then we got in the car and drove along.

"Ever seen any buffalo, Hank?" gramps asked me.

"No, Wally, I haven't."

I called him "Wally." Old whiskey buddies. Like hell.

"We have them here."

"I thought they were just about extinct?"

"Oh, no, we got dozens of 'em."

"I don't believe it."

"Show him, Daddy Wally," said Joyce.

Silly bitch. She called him "Daddy Wally." He wasn't her daddy.

"All right."

We drove on a way until we came to this empty fenced-in field. The ground sloped and you couldn't see the other end of the field. It was miles long and wide. There was nothing but short green grass.

"I don't see any buffalo," I said.

"The wind's right," said Wally. "Just climb in there and walk a ways. You've got to walk a ways to see them."

There was nothing in field. They thought they were being very funny, conning a city-slicker. I climbed the fence and walked on in.

"Well, where are the buffalo?" I called back.

"They're there. Go on in."

Oh hell, they were going to play the old drive-away joke. Damned farmers. They'd wait until I got in there and then drive off laughing. Well, let them. I could walk back. It'd give me a rest from Joyce.

I walked very quickly into the field, waiting for them to drive off. I didn't hear them leaving. I walked further in, then turned, cupped my hands and yelled back at them: "WELL, WHERE'S THE BUFFALO?"

My answer came from behind me. I could hear their feet on the ground. There were 3 of them, big ones, just like in the movies, and they were running, they were coming FAST! One had a bit of a lead on the others. There was little doubt who they were headed for.

"Oh shit!" I said.

I turned and began running. That fence looked a long way away. It looked impossible. I couldn't spare the time to look back. That might make the difference. I was flying, wide-eyed. I really moved! But they gained steadily! I could feel the ground shaking around me as they beat up earth getting right down on me. I could hear them slobbering, I could hear them breathing. With the last of my strength I dug in and leaped the fence. I didn't climb it. I sailed over it. And landed on my back in a ditch with one of those things poking his head over the fence and looking down at me.

In the car, they were all laughing. They thought it was the funniest thing they had ever seen. Joyce was laughing louder than any of them.

The stupid beasts circled, then loped off.

I got out of the ditch and climbed in the car.

"I've seen the buffalo," I said, "now let's go catch a drink."

They laughed all the way in. They'd stop and then somebody would start and then they all would start. Wally had to stop the car once. He couldn't drive anymore. He opened the door and rolled out on the ground and laughed. Even grandma was getting hers, along with Joyce.

Later the story got around in town and there was a bit of swagger missing from my walk. I needed a haircut. I told Joyce.

She said, "Go to a barbershop."

And I said, "I can't. It's the buffalo."

"Are you afraid of those men in the barbershop?"

"It's the buffalo," I said.

Joyce cut my hair.

She did a terrible job.

# 4

THEN JOYCE WANTED to go back to the city. For all the drawbacks, that little town, haircuts or not, beat city life. It was quiet. We had our own house. Joyce fed me well. Plenty of meat. Rich, good, well-cooked meat. I'll say one thing for that bitch. She could cook. She could cook better than any woman I had ever known. Food is good for the

nerves and the spirit. Courage comes from the belly—all
else is desperation.

But no, she wanted to go. Granny was always climbing
her and she was pissed. Me, I rather enjoyed playing the
villain. I had made her cousin, the town bully, back down.
It had never been done before. On blue jean day everybody
in town was supposed to wear blue jeans or get thrown in
the lake. I put on my only suit and necktie and slowly, like
Billy the Kid, with all eyes on me, I walked slowly through
the town, looking in windows, stopping for cigars. I broke
that town in half like a wooden match.

Later, I met the town doctor in the street. I liked him.
He was always high on drugs. I was not a drug man, but
in case I had to hide from myself for a few days, I knew I
could get anything I wanted from him.

"We've got to leave," I told him.

"You ought to stay here," he said, "it's a good life.
Plenty of hunting and fishing. The air's good. And no
pressure. You own this town," he said.

"I know, doc, but she wears the pants."

# 5

So GRAMPS WROTE Joyce a big check and there we were.
We rented a little house up on a hill, and then Joyce got
this stupid moralistic thing.

"We both ought to get jobs," Joyce said, "to prove to
them that you are not after their money. To prove to them
that we are self-sufficient."

"Baby, that's grammar school. Any damn fool can beg
up some kind of job; it takes a wise man to make it without
working. Out here we call it 'hustling.' I'd like to be a good
hustler."

She didn't want it.

Then I explained that a man couldn't find a job unless he had a car to drive around in. Joyce got on the phone and gramps sent the money on in. Next thing I knew I was sitting in a new Plymouth. She sent me out on the streets dressed in a fine new suit, 40 dollar shoes, and I thought, what the hell, I'll try to stretch it out. Shipping clerk, that's what I was. When you didn't know how to do anything that's what you become—a shipping clerk, receiving clerk, stock boy. I checked two ads, went to two places and both of the places hired me. The first place smelled like work, so I took the second.

So there I was with my gummed tape machine working in an art store. It was easy. There was only an hour or two of work a day. I listened to the radio, built a little office out of plywood, put an old desk in there, the telephone, and I sat around reading the Racing Form. I'd get bored sometimes and walk down the alley to the coffee shop and sit in there, drinking coffee, eating pie and flirting with the waitresses.

The truck drivers would come in:

"Where's Chinaski?"

"He's down at the coffeeshop."

They'd come down there, have a coffee, and then we'd walk up the alley and do our bit, take a few cartons off the truck or throw them on. Something about a bill of lading.

They wouldn't fire me. Even the salesmen liked me. They were robbing the boss out the back door but I didn't say anything. That was their little game. It didn't interest me. I wasn't much of a petty thief. I wanted the whole world or nothing.

# 6

THERE WAS DEATH in that place on the hill. I knew it the first day I walked out the screen door and into the backyard. A zinging binging buzzing whining sound came right at me: 10,000 flies rose straight up into the air at once. All the backyards had these flies—there was this tall green grass and they nested in it, they loved it.

Oh Jesus Christ, I thought, and not a spider within 5 miles!

As I stood there, the 10,000 flies began to come down out of the sky, settling down in the grass, along the fence, the ground, in my hair, on my arms, everywhere. One of the bolder ones bit me.

I cursed, ran out and bought the biggest fly sprayer you ever saw. I fought them for hours, raging we were, the flies and I, and hours later, coughing and sick from breathing the fly killer, I looked around and there were as many flies as ever. I think for each one I killed they got down in the grass and bred two. I gave it up.

The bedroom had this room-break encircling the bed. There were pots and the pots had geraniums in them. When I went to bed with Joyce the first time and we worked out, I noticed the boards begin to wave and shake.

Then plop.

"Oh, oh!" I said.

"What's the matter now?" asked Joyce. "Don't stop! Don't stop!"

"Baby, a pot of geraniums just fell on my ass."

"Don't stop! Go ahead!"

"All right, all right!"

I stoked up again, was going fairly well, then—

"Oh, shit!"

"What is it? What is it?"

"Another pot of geraniums, baby, hit me in the small of the back, rolled down my back to my ass, then dropped off."

"God *damn* the geraniums! Go ahead! Go ahead!"

"Oh, all right . . ."

All through the workout these pots kept falling down on me. It was like trying to screw during an aerial attack. I finally made it.

Later I said, "Look, baby, we've got to do something about those geraniums."

"No, you leave them there!"

"Why, baby, why?"

"It adds to it."

"It adds to it?"

"Yes."

She just giggled. But the pots stayed up there. Most of the time.

# 7

THEN I STARTED coming home unhappy.

"What's the matter, Hank?"

I had to get drunk every night.

"It's the manager, Freddy. He has started whistling this song. He's whistling it when I come in in the morning and he never stops, and he's whistling it when I go home at night. It's been going on for two weeks!"

"What's the name of the song?"

"*Around The World In Eighty Days*. I never did like that song."

"Well, get another job."

"I will."

"But keep working there until you find another job. We've got to prove to them that . . ."

"All right. All right!"

# 8

I MET AN old drunk on the street one afternoon. I used to know him from the days with Betty when we made the rounds of the bars. He told me that he was now a postal clerk and that there was nothing to the job.

It was one of the biggest fattest lies of the century. I've been looking for that guy for years but I'm afraid somebody else has gotten to him first.

So there I was taking the civil service exam again. Only this time I marked the paper "clerk" instead of "carrier."

By the time I got the notice to report for the swearing-in ceremonies, Freddy had stopped whistling *Around The World In Eighty Days*, but I was looking forward to that soft job with "Uncle Sam."

I told Freddy, "I've got a little business to take care of, so I may take an hour or an hour and a half for lunch."

"O.K., Hank."

Little did I know how long that lunch would be.

# 9

THERE WAS A gang of us down there. 150 or 200. There were tedious papers to fill out. Then we all stood up and faced the flag. The guy who swore us in was the same guy who had sworn me in before.

After swearing us in, the guy told us:

"All right now, you've got a good job. Keep your nose clean and you've got the security the rest of your life."

Security? You could get security in jail. 3 squares and no rent to pay, no utilities, no income tax, no child support. No license plate fees. No traffic tickets. No drunk driving raps. No losses at the race track. Free medical attention.

Comradeship with those with similar interests. Church. Round-eye. Free burial.

Nearly 12 years later, out of these 150 or 200, there would only be 2 of us left. Just like some guys can't taxi or pimp or hustle dope, most guys, and gals too, can't be postal clerks. And I don't blame them. As the years went by, I saw them continue to march in their squads of 150 or 200 and two, three, or four remain out of each group—just enough to replace those who were retiring.

## 10

THE GUIDE TOOK us all over the building. There were so many of us that they had to break us up into groups. We used the elevator in shifts. We were shown the employees' cafeteria, the basement, all those dull things.

God o mighty, I thought, I wish he'd hurry up. My lunch is over two hours late now.

Then the guide handed us all timecards. He showed us the timeclocks.

"Now here is how you punch in."

He showed us how. Then he said, "Now, you punch in."

Twelve and one half hours later we punched out. That was one hell of a swearing-in ceremony.

## 11

AFTER NINE OR ten hours people began getting sleepy and falling into their cases, catching themselves just in time. We were working the zoned mail. If a letter read zone 28 you stuck it to hole no. 28. It was simple.

One big black guy leaped up and began swinging his arms to keep awake. He staggered about the floor.

"God damn! I can't *stand* it!" he said.

And he was a big powerful brute. Using the same muscles over and over again was quite tiring. I ached all over. And at the end of the aisle stood a supervisor, another Stone, and he had this *look* on his face—they must practice it in front of mirrors, all the supervisors had this *look* on their faces—they looked at you as if you were a hunk of human shit. Yet they had come in through the same door. They had once been clerks or carriers. I couldn't understand it. They were handpicked screws.

You had to keep one foot on the floor at all times. One notch up on the rest-bar. What they called a "rest-bar" was a little round cushion set up on a stilt. No talking allowed. Two 10 minute breaks in 8 hours. They wrote down the time when you left and the time when you came back. If you stayed 12 or 13 minutes, you heard about it.

But the pay was better than at the art store. And, I thought, I might get used to it.

# 12

THEN THE SUPERVISOR moved us to a new aisle. We had been there ten hours.

"Before you begin," the soup said, "I want to tell you something. Each tray of this type of mail must be stuck in 23 minutes. That's the production schedule. Now, just for fun, let's see if each of us can meet the production schedule! Now, one, two, three . . . GO!"

What the hell is this? I thought. I'm tired.

Each tray was two feet long. But each tray held different amounts of letters. Some trays had 2 or 3 times as much mail in them as others, depending upon the size of the letters.

Arms started flying. Fear of failure.

I took my time.

"When you finish your first tray, grab another!"

They really worked at it. Then they jumped up and grabbed another tray.

The supervisor walked up behind me. "Now," he said, pointing at me, "*this* man is making production. He's half-way through his second tray!"

It was my first tray. I didn't know if he were trying to con me or not, but since I was that far ahead of them I slowed down a little more.

# 13

AT 3:30 A.M. MY twelve hours were up. At that time they did not pay the subs time and one half for overtime. You just got straight time. And you hired in as a "temporary indefinite substitute clerk."

I set the alarm so that I would be at the art store at 8 a.m.

"What happened, Hank? We thought maybe you had been in an auto accident. We kept waiting for you to come back."

"I'm quitting."

"Quitting?"

"Yes, you can't blame a man for wanting to better himself."

I walked into the office and got my check. I was back in the post office again.

# 14

MEANWHILE, THERE WAS still Joyce, and her geraniums, and a couple of million if I could hang on. Joyce and the flies and the geraniums. I worked the night shift, 12 hours, and she pawed me during the day, trying to get me to perform. I'd be asleep and I'd awaken with this hand stroking me. Then I'd have to do it. The poor dear was mad.

Then I came in one morning and she said, "Hank, don't be mad."

I was too tired to be mad.

"What izzit, baby?"

"I got us a dog. A little pup dog."

"O.K. That's nice. There's nothing wrong with dogs. Where is he?"

"He's in the kitchen. I named him 'Picasso.' "

I walked in and looked at the dog. He couldn't see. Hair covered his eyes. I watched him walk. Then I picked him up and looked at his eyes. Poor Picasso!

"Baby, you know what you've gone and done?"

"You don't like him?"

"I didn't say I didn't like him. But he's a subnormal. He has an I.Q. of about 12. You've gone and gotten us an idiot of a dog."

"How can you tell?"

"I can tell just by looking at him."

Just then Picasso started to piss. Picasso was full of piss. It ran in long yellow rivulets along the kitchen floor. Then Picasso finished, ran and looked at it.

I picked him up.

"Mop it up."

So Picasso was just one more problem.

I'd awaken after a 12 hour night with Joyce strumming me under the geraniums and I'd say, "Where's Picasso?"

"Oh god *damn* Picasso!" she'd say.

I'd get out of bed, naked, with this big thing in front of me.

"Look, you've left him out in the yard again! I *told* you not to leave him out in the yard in the daytime!"

Then I'd go out into the backyard, naked, too tired to dress. It was fairly well sheltered. And there would be poor Picasso, overrun with 500 flies, flies crawling all over him in circles. I'd run out with the thing (going down then) and curse those flies. They were in his eyes, under the hair, in his ears, on his privates, in his mouth . . . everywhere. And he'd just sit there and smile at me. Laugh at me, while the flies ate him up. Maybe he knew more than any of us. I'd pick him up and carry him into the house.

*"The little dog laughed*
*To see such sport;*
*And the dish ran away with the spoon."*

"God damn it, Joyce! I've told you and told you and told you."

"Well, *you* were the one who housebroke him. He's got to go out there to crap!"

"Yes, but when he's through, bring him in. He doesn't have sense enough to come in himself. And wash away the crap when he's finished. You're creating a fly-paradise out there."

Then as soon as I fell asleep, Joyce would begin stroking me again. That couple of million was a long time coming.

# 15

I WAS HALF asleep in a chair, waiting for a meal.

I got up for a glass of water and as I walked into the kitchen I saw Picasso walk up to Joyce and lick her ankle. I was barefooted and she didn't hear me. She had on high heels. She looked at him and her face was pure smalltown hatred, white hot. She kicked him hard in the side with the point of her shoe. The poor fellow just ran in little circles, whimpering. Piss dripped from his bladder. I walked in for my glass of water. I held the glass in my hand and then before I could get the water into it I threw the glass at the cupboard to the left of the sink. Glass went everywhere. Joyce had time to cover her face. I didn't bother. I picked up the dog and walked out. I sat in the chair with him and petted the little shitsnot. He looked up at me and his tongue came out and licked my wrist. His tail wagged and flapped like a fish dying in a sack.

I saw Joyce on her knees with a paper sack, gathering glass. Then she began to sob. She tried to hide it. She turned her back to me but I could see the jolts of it, shaking her, tearing her.

I put Picasso down and walked into the kitchen.

"Baby. Baby, *don't!*"

I picked her up from behind. She was limp.

"Baby, I'm sorry . . . I'm *sorry*."

I held her up against me, my hand flat on her belly. I rubbed her belly easily and gently, trying to stop the convulsions.

Easy, baby, easy now. Easy . . .

She quieted a little. I pulled her hair back and kissed her behind the ear. It was warm back there. She jerked her head away. The next time I kissed her there she didn't jerk her head away. I could feel her inhale, then she let out a little moan. I picked her up and carried her to the other room, sat down in a chair with her in my lap. She wouldn't look at me. I kissed her throat and ears. One hand around her shoulders and the other above the hip. I moved the hand above her hip up and down with her breathing, trying to work the bad electricity out.

Finally, with the faintest of smiles, she looked at me. I reached out and bit the point of her chin.

"Crazy bitch!" I said.

She laughed and then we kissed, our heads moving back and forth. She began to sob again.

I pulled back and said, "DON'T!"

We kissed again. Then I picked her up and carried her to the bedroom, placed her on the bed, got my pants and shorts and shoes off *fast*, pulled her pants down over her shoes, got one of the shoes off, and then with one shoe off and one on, I gave her the best ride in months. Every geranium plant shook off the boards. When I finished, I nursed her back slowly, playing with her long hair, telling her things. She purred. Finally she got up and went to the bathroom.

She didn't come back. She went into the kitchen and began washing dishes and singing.

For Christ's sake, Steve McQueen couldn't have done better.

I had two Picassos on my hands.

# 16

AFTER DINNER OR lunch or whatever it was—with my crazy 12 hour night I was no longer sure what was what—I said, "Look, baby, I'm sorry, but don't you realize that this job is driving me crazy? Look, let's give it up. Let's just lay around and make love and take walks and talk a little. Let's go to the zoo. Let's look at animals. Let's drive down and look at the ocean. It's only 45 minutes. Let's play games in the arcades. Let's go to the races, the Art Museum, the boxing matches. Let's have friends. Let's laugh. This kind of life is like everybody else's kind of life: it's killing us."

"No, Hank, we've got to show them, we've got to show them . . ."

It was the little smalltown Texas girl speaking.
I gave it up.

# 17

EACH NIGHT AS I got ready to go in, Joyce had my clothing laid out on the bed. Everything was the most expensive money could buy. I never wore the same pair of pants, the same shirt, the same shoes two nights in a row. There were dozens of different outfits. I put on whatever she laid out for me. Just like mama used to do.

I haven't come very far, I thought, and then I'd put the stuff on.

They had this thing called Training Class, and so for 30 minutes each night, anyhow, we didn't have to stick mail.

A big Italiano got up on the lecture platform to tell us where it was.

". . . now there's nothing like the smell of good clean sweat but there's nothing worse than the smell of stale sweat . . ."

Good god, I thought, am I hearing right? This thing is government sanctioned, surely. This big oaf is telling me to wash under the armpits. They wouldn't do this to an engineer or a concert-master. He's downgrading us.

". . . so take a bath everyday. You will be graded upon appearance as well as production."

I think he wanted to use the word "hygienics" somewhere but it simply wasn't in him.

Then he went to the back of the lecture room and pulled down a big map. And I mean big. It covered half the stage. A light was shone upon the map. And the big Italiano took a pointer with the little rubber nipple on the end of it like they used in grammar school and he pointed to the map:

"Now, you see all this GREEN? Well, there's a hell of a lot of it. Look!"

He took the pointer and rubbed it back and forth along the green.

There was quite a bit more anti-Russian feeling then than there is now. China had not yet begun to flex her muscles. Vietnam was just a little firecracker party. But I still thought, I must be crazy! I can't be hearing right? But nobody in the audience protested. They needed jobs. And according to Joyce, I needed a job.

Then he said, "Look here. That's *Alaska!* And there *they* are! Looks almost as if they could jump across, doesn't it?"

"Yeah," said some brainwash job in the front row.

The Italiano flipped the map. It leaped crisply up into itself, crackling in war fury.

Then he walked to the front of the stage, pointed his rubbertitted pointer at us.

"I want you to understand that we've got to hold down the budget! I want you to understand that EACH LETTER YOU STICK—EACH SECOND, EACH MINUTE, EACH HOUR, EACH DAY, EACH WEEK—EACH EXTRA LETTER YOU STICK BEYOND DUTY HELPS DEFEAT THE RUSSIANS! Now, that's all for today. Before you leave, each of you will receive your scheme assignment."

Scheme assignment. What was that?

Somebody came along handing out these sheets.

"Chinaski?" he said.

"Yeh?"

"You have zone 9."

"Thank you," I said.

I didn't realize what I was saying. Zone 9 was the largest station in the city. Some guys got tiny zones. It was the same as the two foot tray in 23 minutes—they just rammed it into you.

# 19

THE NEXT NIGHT as they moved the group from the main building to the training building, I stopped to talk to Gus the old newsboy. Gus had once been 3rd-ranked welterweight contender but he never got a look at the champ. He swung from the left side, and, as you know, nobody ever likes to fight a lefty—you've got to train your boy all over again. Why bother? Gus took me inside and we had a little nip from his bottle. Then I tried to catch the group.

The Italiano was waiting in the doorway. He saw me coming. He met me halfway in the yard.

"Chinaski?"

"Yeh?"

"You're late."

I didn't say anything. We walked toward the building together.

"I've got half a mind to slap your wrist with a warning slip," he said.

"Oh, *please* don't do that, sir! *Please* don't!" I said as we walked along.

"All right," he said, "I'll let you go this time."

"Thank you, sir," I said, and we walked in together.

Want to know something? The son of a bitch had body odor.

# 20

OUR 30 MINUTES was now devoted to scheme training. They gave us each a deck of cards to learn and stick into our cases. To pass the scheme you had to throw 100 cards in 8 minutes or less with at least 95 per cent accuracy. You were given 3 chances to pass, and if you failed the 3rd time, they let you go. I mean, you were fired.

"Some of you won't make it," the Italiano said. "So maybe you were meant for something else. Maybe you will end up President of General Motors."

Then we were rid of Italiano and we had our nice little scheme instructor who encouraged us.

"You can do it, fellows, it's not as hard as it looks."

Each group had its own scheme instructor and they were graded too, upon the percentage of their group that passed. We had the guy with the lowest percentage. He was worried.

"There's nothing to it, fellows, just put your minds to it."

Some of the fellows had thin decks. I had the fattest deck of them all.

I just stood there in my fancy new clothes. Stood there with my hands in my pockets.

"Chinaski, what's the matter?" the instructor asked. "I know *you* can do it."

"Yeh. Yeh. I'm thinking right now."

"What are you thinking about?"

"Nothing."

And then I walked away.

A week later I was still standing there with my hands in my pockets and a sub walked up to me.

"Sir, I think that I am ready to throw my scheme now."

"Are you sure?" I asked him.

"I've been throwing 97, 98, 99 and a couple of 100's in my practice schemes."

"You must understand that we spend a great deal of money training you. We want you to have this thing down to the ace!"

"Sir, I truly believe that I am ready!"

"All right," I reached out and shook his hand, "go to it then, my boy, and the best of luck."

61

"Thank you, sir."

He ran off towards the scheme room, a glass-enclosed fishbowl they put you in to see if you could swim their waters. Poor fish. What a comedown from being a small-town villain. I walked into the practice room, took the rubber band off of the cards and looked at them for the first time.

"Oh, shit!" I said.

A couple of the guys laughed. Then the scheme instructor said, "Your 30 minutes are up. You will now return to the workfloor."

Which meant back to the 12 hours.

They couldn't keep enough help to get the mail out, so those who did remain had to do it all. On the schedule board they had us working two weeks straight but then we would get 4 days off. That kept us going. 4 days rest. The last night before our 4 days off, the intercom came on.

"ATTENTION! ALL SUBS IN GROUP 409! . . ."

I was in group 409.

". . . YOUR FOUR OFF DAYS HAVE BEEN CAN-CELLED. YOU ARE SCHEDULED TO REPORT FOR WORK ON THESE 4 DAYS!"

# 21

JOYCE FOUND A job with the county, the county Police Department, of all things. I was living with a cop! But at least it was during the day, which gave me a little rest from those fondling hands except—Joyce bought two parakeets, and the damn things didn't talk, they just made these sounds all day.

Joyce and I met over breakfast and dinner—it was all very brisk—nice that way. Though she still managed to rape me now and then, it beat the other, except—the parakeets.

"Look, baby . . ."

"Now what is it?"

"All right. I've gotten used to the geraniums and the flies and Picasso, but you've got to realize that I am working 12 hours a night and studying a scheme on the side, and you molest my remaining energy . . ."

"Molest?"

"All right. I'm not saying it right. I'm sorry."

"What do you mean, 'molest'?"

"I said, forget it! Now look, it's the parakeets."

"So now it's the parakeets! Are they molesting you too?"

"Yes, they are."

"Who's on top?"

"Look, don't get funny. Don't get dirty. I'm trying to tell you something."

"Now you're trying to tell me how to get!"

"All right! *Shit! You're* the one with the money! Are you going to let me talk or not? Answer me, yes or no?"

"All right, little baby: yes."

"All right. Little baby says this: 'Mama! Mama! Those fucking parakeets are driving me nuts!' "

"All right, tell mama how the parakeets are driving you nuts."

"Well, it's like this, mama, the things chatter all day, they never stop, and I keep waiting for them to say something but they never say anything and I can't sleep all day from listening to the idiots!"

"All right, little baby. If they keep you awake, put them out."

"Put them out, mama?"

"Yes, put them out."

"All right, mama."

She gave me a kiss and then wiggled down the stairway on her way to her cop job.

I got into bed and tried to sleep. How they chattered! Every muscle in my body ached. If I lay on this side, if I lay on that side, if I lay on my back, I ached. I found the easiest way was on my stomach, but that grew tiresome. It took a good two or three minutes to get from one position to another.

I tossed and turned, cursing, screaming a little, and laughing a little too, at the ridiculousness of it. On they chattered. They got to me. What did they know of pain in their little cage? Eggheads yakking! Just feathers; brains the size of a pinhead.

I managed to get out of bed, go into the kitchen, fill a cup with water and then I walked up to the cage and threw the water all over them.

"Motherfuckers!" I cursed them.

They looked out at me balefully from under their wet feathers. They were *silent!* Nothing like the old water treatment. I had borrowed a page from the headshrinkers.

Then the green one with the yellow breast reached down and bit himself on the chest. Then he looked up and started chattering to the red one with the green breast, and then they were going again.

I sat on the edge of the bed and listened to them. Picasso walked up and bit me on the ankle.

That did it. I took the cage outside. Picasso followed me. 10,000 flies rose straight up into the air. I put the cage on the ground, opened the cage door and sat on the steps.

Both birds looked at that cage door. They couldn't understand it and they could. I could feel their tiny minds trying to function. They had their food and water right there, but what was that open space?

The green one with the yellow breast went first. He leaped down to the opening from his rung. He sat gripping the wire. He looked around at the flies. He stood there 15 seconds, trying to decide. Then something clicked in his little head. Or her little head. He didn't fly. He shot straight up into the sky. Up, up, up, up. Straight up! Straight up as an arrow! Picasso and I sat there and watched. The damn thing was gone.

Then it was the red one with the green breast's turn.

The red one was much more hesitant. It was a hell of a decision. Humans, birds, everything has to make these decisions. It was a hard game.

So old red walked around thinking it over. Yellow sunlight. Buzzing flies. Man and dog looking on. All that sky, all that sky.

It was too much. Old red leaped to the wire. 3 seconds. ZOOP!

The bird was gone.

Picasso and I picked up the empty cage and walked back into the house.

I HAD a good sleep for the first time in weeks. I even forgot to set the alarm. I was riding a white horse down Broadway, New York City. I had just been elected mayor. I had this big hard-on, and then somebody threw a hunk of mud at me . . . and Joyce shook me.

"What happened to the birds?"

"Damn the birds! I am the mayor of New York!"

"I asked you about the birds! All I see is an empty cage!"

"Birds? Birds? What birds?"

"Wake up, damn you!"

"Hard day at the office dear? You seem snappish."

"Where ARE the BIRDS?"

"You said to put them out if they kept me awake."

"I meant to put them in the back porch or outside, you fool!"

"Fool?"

"Yes, you fool! Do you mean to say you let those birds out of the cage? Do you mean to say that you really let them out of the cage?"

"Well, all I can say is, they are not locked in the bathroom, they are not in the cupboard."

"They'll starve out there!"

"They can catch worms, eat berries, all that stuff."

"They can't, they can't. They don't know how! They'll die!"

"Let 'em learn or let 'em die," I said, and then I turned slowly over and went back to sleep. Vaguely, I could hear her cooking her dinner, dropping lids and spoons on the floor, cursing. But Picasso was on the bed with me. Picasso was safe from her sharp shoes. I put my hand out and he licked it and then I slept.

That is, I did for a while. Next thing I knew I was being fondled. I looked up and she was staring into my eyes like a madwoman. She was naked, her breasts dangling in my eyes. Her hair tickling my nostrils. I thought of her millions, picked her up, flipped her on her back and stuck it in.

## 22

SHE WASN'T REALLY a cop, she was a clerk-cop. And she started coming in and telling me about a guy who wore a purple stick pin and was a "real gentleman."

"Oh, he's so *kind!*"

I heard all about him each night.

"Well," I'd ask, "how was old Purple Stickpin tonight?"

"Oh," she said, "you know what happened?"

"No, babe, that's why I'm asking."

"Oh, he's SUCH a gentleman!"

"All right. All right. What happened?"

"You know, he has *suffered* so much!"

"Of course."

"His wife died, you know."

"No, I didn't."

"Don't be so flip. I'm telling you, his wife died and it cost him 15 thousand dollars in medical and burial bills."

"All right. So?"

"I was walking down the hall. He was coming the other way. We met. He looked at me, and with this Turkish accent he said, 'Ah, you are so beautiful!' And you know what he did?"

"No, babe, tell me. Tell me quick."

"He kissed me on the forehead, lightly, ever so lightly. And then he walked on."

"I can tell you something about him, babe. He's seen too many movies."

"How did you know?"

"Whatcha mean?"

"He owns a drive-in theatre. He operates it after work each night."

"That figures," I said.

"But he's *such* a gentleman!" she said.

"Look, babe, I don't want to hurt you, but—"

"But what?"

"Look, you're small-town. I've had over 50 jobs, maybe a hundred. I've never stayed anywhere long. What I am trying to say is, there is a certain game played in offices all over America. The people are bored, they don't know what to do, so they play the office-romance game. Most of the time it means nothing but the passing of time. Sometimes they do manage to work off a screw or two on the side. But even then, it is just an offhand past-time, like bowling or t.v. or a New Year's eve party. You've got to understand that it doesn't mean anything and then you won't get hurt. Do you understand what I mean?"

"I think that Mr. Partisian is sincere."

"You're going to get stuck with that pin, babe, don't forget I told you. Watch those slicks. They are as phony as a lead dime."

"He's not phony. He's a gentleman. He's a real gentleman. I wish you were a gentleman."

I gave it up. I sat on the couch and took my scheme sheet and tried to memorize Babcock Boulevard. Babcock broke: 14, 39, 51, 62. What the hell? Couldn't I remember that?

# 23

I FINALLY GOT a day off, and you know what I did? I got up early before Joyce got back in and I went down to the market to do a little shopping, and maybe I was crazy. I walked through the market and instead of getting a nice red steak or even a bit of frying chicken, you know what I did? I hit snake-eyes and walked over to the Oriental section and began filling my basket full of octopi, sea-spiders, snails, seaweed and so forth. The clerk gave me a strange look and began ringing it up.

When Joyce came home that night, I had it all on the table, ready. Cooked seaweed mixed with a dash of sea-spider, and piles of little golden, fried-in-butter snails.

I took her into the kitchen and showed her the stuff on the table.

"I've cooked this in your honor," I said, "in dedication of our love."

"What the hell's that shit?" she asked,

"Snails."

"Snails?"

"Yes, don't you realise that for many centuries Orientals have thrived upon this and the like? Let us honor them and honor ourselves. It's fried in butter."

Joyce came in and sat down.

I started snapping snails into my mouth.

"God damn, they are good, baby! TRY ONE!"

Joyce reached down and forked one into her mouth while looking at the others on her plate.

I jammed in a big mouthful of delicious seaweed. "Good, huh, baby?"

She chewed the snail in her mouth.

"Fried in golden butter!"

I picked up a few with my hand, tossed them into my mouth.

"The centuries are on our side, babe. We can't go wrong!"

She finally swallowed hers. Then examined the others on her plate.

"They all have tiny little *assholes!* It's horrible! Horrible!"

"What's horrible about assholes, baby?"

She held a napkin to her mouth. Got up and ran to the bathroom. She began vomiting. I hollered in from the kitchen:

"WHAT'S WRONG WITH ASSHOLES, BABY? YOU'VE GOT AN ASSHOLE, I'VE GOT AN ASS-HOLE! YOU GO TO THE STORE AND BUY A PORTERHOUSE STEAK, THAT HAD AN ASS-HOLE! ASSHOLES COVER THE EARTH! IN A WAY TREES HAVE ASSHOLES BUT YOU CAN'T FIND THEM, THEY JUST DROP THEIR LEAVES. YOUR ASSHOLE, MY ASSHOLE, THE WORLD IS FULL OF BILLIONS OF ASSHOLES, THE PRESIDENT HAS AN ASSHOLE, THE CARWASH BOY HAS AN

69

ASSHOLE, THE JUDGE AND THE MURDERER HAVE ASSHOLES ... EVEN PURPLE STICKPIN HAS AN ASSHOLE!"

"Oh stop it! STOP IT!"

She heaved again. Small town. I opened the bottle of sake and had a drink.

## 24

IT WAS ABOUT a week later around 7 a.m. I had lucked into another day off and after a double workout, I was up against Joyce's ass, her asshole, sleeping, verily sleeping, and then the doorbell rang and I got out of bed and answered the thing.

There was a small man in a necktie. He jammed some papers into my hand and ran away.

It was a summons, for divorce. There went my millions. But I wasn't angry because I had never expected her millions anyhow.

I awakened Joyce.

"What?"

"Couldn't you have had me awakened at a more decent hour?"

I showed her the papers.

"I'm sorry, Hank."

"That's O.K. All you had to do was tell me. I would have agreed. We just made love twice and laughed and had fun. I don't understand it. And you knew all along. God damn if I can understand a woman."

"Look, I filed when we had an argument. I thought, if I wait until I cool off I'll never do it."

"O.K., babe, I admire an honest woman. Is it Purple Stickpin?"

"It's Purple Stickpin," she said.

I laughed. It was a rather sad laugh, I'll admit. But it came out.

"It's easy to second guess. But you're going to have trouble with him. I wish you luck, babe. You know there's a lot of you I've loved and it hasn't been entirely your money."

She began to cry into the pillow, on her stomach, shaking all over. She was just a small town girl, spoiled and mixed-up. There she shook, crying, nothing fake about it. It was terrible.

The blankets had fallen off and I stared down at her white back, the shoulder blades sticking out as if they wanted to grow into wings, poke through that skin. Little blades. She was helpless.

I got into bed, stroked her back, stroked her, stroked her, calmed her—then she'd break down again:

"Oh Hank, I love you, I love you, I'm so sorry, I'm so sorry sorry so sorry!"

She was really on the rack.

After a while, I began to feel as if I were the one who was divorcing *her*.

Then we knocked off a good one for old time's sake.

She got the place, the dog, the flies, the geraniums.

She even helped me pack. Folding my pants neatly into suitcases. Packing in my shorts and razor. When I was ready to leave she started crying again. I bit her on the ear, the right one, then went down the stairway with my stuff. I got into the car and began cruising up and down the streets looking for a For Rent sign.

It didn't seem to be an unusual thing to do.

# III

## 1

I DIDN'T CONTEST the divorce, didn't go to court. Joyce gave me the car. She didn't drive. All I had lost was 3 or 4 million. But I still had the post office.

I met Betty on the street.

"I saw you with that bitch a while back. She's not your kind of woman."

"None of them are."

I told her it was over. We went for a beer. Betty had gotten old, fast. Heavier. The lines had come in. Flesh hung under the throat. It was sad. But I had gotten old too.

Betty had lost her job. The dog had been run over and killed. She got a job as a waitress, then lost that when they tore down the cafe to erect an office building. Now she lived in a small room in a loser's hotel. She changed the sheets there and cleaned the bathrooms. She was on wine. She suggested that we might get together again. I suggested that we might wait awhile. I was just getting over a bad one.

She went back to her room and put on her best dress, high heels, tried to fix up. But there was a terrible sadness about her.

We got a fifth of whiskey and some beer, went up to my place on the 4th floor of an old apartment house. I picked up the phone and called in sick. I sat across from Betty. She crossed her legs, kicked her heels, laughed a little. It was like old times. Almost. Something was missing.

At that time, when you called in sick the post office sent out a nurse to spot check, to make sure you weren't night-clubbing or sitting in a poker parlor. My place was close to the central office, so it was convenient for them to check up on me. Betty and I had been there about two hours when there was a knock on the door.

"What's that?"

"All right," I whispered, "shut up! Take off those high heels, go into the kitchen and don't make a sound."

"JUST A MOMENT!" I answered the knocker.

I lit a cigarette to kill my breath, then went to the door and opened it a notch. It was the nurse. The same one. She knew me.

"Now what's your trouble?" she asked.

I blew out a little roll of smoke.

"Upset stomach."

"Are you sure?"

"It's my stomach."

"Will you sign this form to show that I called here and that you were at home?"

"Surely."

The nurse slipped the form in sideways. I signed it. Slipped it back out.

"Will you be in to work tomorrow?"

"I have no way of knowing. If I'm well, I'll come in. If not, I'll stay out."

She gave me a dirty look and walked off. I knew she had smelled whiskey on my breath. Proof enough? Probably not, too many technicalities, or maybe she was laughing as she got into her car with her little black bag.

"All right," I said, "get on your shoes and come on out."

"Who was it?"

"A post office nurse."

"Is she gone?"

"Yeh."

"Do they do that all the time?"

"They haven't missed yet. Now let's each have a good tall drink to celebrate!"

I walked into the kitchen and poured 2 good ones. I came out and handed Betty her drink.

"Salud!" I said.

We raised our glasses high, clicked them.

Then the *alarm* clock went off and it was a loud one.

I jerked as if I had been shot in the back. Betty leaped a foot into the air, straight up. I ran over to the clock and shut off the alarm.

"Jesus," she said, "I almost shit myself!"

We both started laughing. Then we sat down. Had the good drink.

"I had a boyfriend who worked for the county," she said. "They used to send out an inspector, a guy, but not everytime, maybe one time in 5. So this night I am drinking with Harry—that was his name: Harry. This night I am drinking with Harry and there's a knock on the door. Harry's sitting on the couch with all his clothes on. 'Oh Jesus Christ!' he says, and he leaps into bed with all his clothes on and pulls the covers up. I put the bottles and glasses under the bed and open the door. This guy comes in and sits on the couch. Harry even has his shoes and stockings on but he is completely under the covers. The guy says, 'How you feeling, Harry?' And Harry says, 'Not so good. She's over to take care of me.' He points to me. I was sitting there drunk. 'Well, I hope you get well, Harry,' the guy says, and then he leaves. I'm sure he saw those bottles and glasses under the bed, and I'm sure he knew that Harry's feet weren't *that* big. It was a jumpy time."

"Damn, they won't let a man live at all, will they? They always want him at the wheel."

"Of course."

We drank a little longer and then we went to bed, but it wasn't the same, it never is—there was space between us, things had happened. I watched her walk to the bathroom, saw the wrinkles and folds under the cheeks of her ass. Poor thing. Poor poor thing. Joyce had been firm and hard—you grabbed a handful and it felt good. Betty didn't feel so good. It was sad, it was sad, it was sad. When Betty came back we didn't sing or laugh, or even argue. We sat drinking in the dark, smoking cigarettes, and when we went to sleep, I didn't put my feet on her body or she on mine like we used to. We slept without touching.

We had both been robbed.

## 2

I PHONED Joyce.

"How's it working with Purple Stickpin?"

"I can't understand it," she said.

"What did he do when you told him you were divorced?"

"We were sitting across from each other in the employee's cafeteria when I told him."

"What happened?"

"He dropped his fork. His mouth fell open. He said, 'What?'"

"He knew you meant business then."

"I can't understand it. He's been avoiding me ever since. When I see him in the hall he runs away. He doesn't sit across from me anymore when we eat. He seems . . . well, almost . . . cold."

"Baby, there are other men. Forget that guy. Set your sails for a new one."

"It's hard to forget him. I mean, the way he was."

"Does he know that you have money?"

"No, I have never told him, he doesn't know."

"Well, if you want him . . ."

"No, no! I don't want him that way!"

"All right, then. Goodbye Joyce."

"Goodbye, Hank."

It wasn't long after that, I got a letter from her. She was back in Texas. Grandma was very sick, she wasn't expected to live long. People were asking about me. So forth. Love, Joyce.

I put the letter down and I could see that midget wondering how I had missed out. Little shaking freak, thinking I was such a clever bastard. It was hard to let him down like that.

Then I was called down to personnel at the old Federal Building. They let me sit the usual 45 minutes or hour and one half.

Then, "Mr. Chinaski?" this voice said.

"Yeh," I said.

"Step in."

The man walked me back to a desk. There sat this woman. She looked a bit sexy, melting into 38 or 39, but she looked as if her sexual ambition had either been laid aside for other things or as if it had been ignored.

"Sit down, Mr. Chinaski."

I sat down.

Baby, I thought, I could really give you a ride.

"Mr. Chinaski," she said, "we have been wondering if you have filled out this application properly."

"Uh?"

"We mean, the arrest record."

She handed me the sheet. There wasn't any sex in her eyes.

I had listed 8 or 10 common drunk raps. It was only an estimate. I had no idea of the dates.

"Now, have you listed *everything?*" she asked me.

"Hmmm, hmmm, let me think . . ."

I knew what she wanted. She wanted me to say "yes" and then she had me.

"Let me see . . . Hmmm. Hmmm."

"Yes?" she said.

"Oh oh! My god!"

"What is it?"

"It's either drunk in auto or drunk driving. About 4 years ago or so. I don't know the exact date."

"And this was a slip of the mind?"

"Yes, really, I meant to put it down."

"All right. Put it down."

I wrote it down.

"Mr. Chinaski. This is a terrible record. I want you to explain these charges and if possible justify your present employment with us."

"All right."

"You have ten days to reply."

I didn't want the job that badly. But she irritated me.

I phoned in sick that night after buying some ruled and numbered legal paper and a blue, very official-looking folder. I got a fifth of whiskey and a six pack, then sat down and typed it out. I had the dictionary at my elbow. Every now and then I would flip a page, find a large incomprehensible word and build a sentence or paragraph out of the idea. It ran 42 pages. I finished up with, "Copies of this statement have been retained for distribution to the press, television, and other mass communication media."

I was full of shit.

*She* got up from her desk and got it personally. "Mr. Chinaski?"

"Yes?"

It was 9 a.m. One day after her request to answer charges. "Just a moment."

She took the 42 pages back to her desk. She read and read and read. There was somebody reading over her shoulder. Then there were 2, 3, 4, 5. All reading. 6, 7, 8, 9. All reading.

What the hell? I thought.

Then I heard a voice from the crowd, "Well, all geniuses are drunkards!" As if that explained away the matter. Too many movies again.

She got up from the desk with the 42 pages in her hand. "Mr. Chinaski?"

"Yes?"

"Your case will be continued. You will hear from us."

"Meanwhile, continue working?"

"Meanwhile, continue working."

"Good morning," I said.

# 4

ONE NIGHT I was assigned to the stool next to Butchner. He didn't stick any mail. He just sat there. And talked.

A young girl came in and sat down at the end of the aisle. I heard Butchner. "Yeah, you cunt! You want my cock in your pussy, don't you? That's what you want, you cunt, don't you?"

I went on sticking mail. The soup walked past. Butchner said, "You're on my list, mother! I'm going to get you, you dirty mother! You rotten bastard! Cocksucker!"

The supervisors never bothered Butchner. Nobody ever bothered Butchner.

Then I heard him again. "All right, babyl I don't like that look on your face! You're on my list, mother! You're right there on top of my list! I'm going to get your ass! Hey, I'm talking to you! You hear me?"

It was too much, I threw my mail down.

"All right," I told him, "I'm calling your card! I'm calling your whole stinking deck! You wanna go right here or outside?"

I looked at Butchner. He was talking to the ceiling, insane:

"I told you, you're on top of my list! I'm going to get you and I'm going to get you good!"

O for Christ's sake, I thought, I really sucked into that one! The clerks were very quiet. I couldn't blame them. I got up, went to get a drink of water. Then came back. 20 minutes later I got up to take my ten minute break. When I got back, the supervisor was waiting. A fat black man in his early 50's. He screamed at me:

"CHINASKI !"

"What's the matter, man?" I asked.

"You've left your seat twice in 30 minutes!"

"Yeah, I got a drink of water the first time. 30 seconds. Then later I took my break."

"Suppose you worked at a machine! You couldn't leave your machine twice in 30 minutes!"

His whole face glistened in fury. It was astounding. I couldn't understand it.

"I'm WRITING YOU UP!"

"All right," I said.

I went down and sat next to Butchner. The supervisor came running down with the write-up. It was written in longhand. I couldn't even read it. He had written in such fury that it had all come out in blots and slants.

I folded the write-up into a neat package, slipped it in my rear pocket.

"I'm going to kill that son of a bitch!" Butchner said.

"I wish you would, fat boy," I said, "I wish you would."

# 5

IT WAS 12 hours a night, plus supervisors, plus clerks, plus the fact that you could hardly breathe in that pack of flesh, plus stale baked food in the "non-profit" cafeteria.

Plus the CP1. City Primary 1. That station scheme was nothing compared to the City Primary 1. Which contained about 1/3 of the streets in the city and how they were broken up into zone numbers. I lived in one of the largest cities in the U.S. That was a lot of streets. After that there was CP2. And CP3. You had to pass each test in 90 days, 3 shots at it, 95 percent or better, 100 cards in a glass cage, 8 minutes, fail and they let you try for President of General Motors, as the man said. For those who got through, the schemes would get a little easier, the 2nd or 3rd time around. But with the 12 hour night and cancelled days off, it was too much for most. Already, out of our original group of 150 to 200, there were only 17 or 18 of us left.

"How can I work 12 hours a night, sleep, eat, bathe, travel back and forth, get the laundry and the gas, the rent, change tires, do all the things that have to be done and still study the scheme?" I asked one of the instructors in the scheme room.

"Do without sleep," he told me.

I looked at him. He wasn't playing *Dixie* on the harmonica. The damn fool was serious.

# 6

I FOUND THAT the only time to study was before sleeping. I was always too tired to make and eat breakfast, so I would go out and buy a tall 6 pack, put it on the chair beside the bed, rip open a can, take a good pull and then open the scheme sheet. About the time I got to the 3rd can of beer I had to drop the sheet. You could only inject so much. Then I'd drink the rest of the beer, sitting up in bed, staring at the walls. With the last can I'd be asleep. And when I awakened, there was just time to toilet, bathe, eat, and drive back on in.

And you didn't adjust, you simply got more and more tired. I always picked up my 6 pack on the way in, and one morning I was really done. I climbed the staircase (there was no elevator) and put the key in. The door swung open. Somebody had changed all the furniture around, put in a new rug. No, the furniture was new too.

There was a woman on the couch. She looked all right. Young. Good legs. A blonde.

"Hello," I said, "care for a beer?"

"Hi!" she said. "All right, I'll have one."

"I like the way this place is fixed up," I told her.

"I did it myself."

"But *why?*"

"I just felt like it," she said.

We each drank at the beer.

"You're all right," I said. I put my beercan down and gave her a kiss. I put my hand on one of her knees. It was a nice knee.

Then I had another swallow of beer.

"Yes," I said, "I really like the way this place looks. It's really going to lift my spirits."

"That's nice. My husband likes it too."

"Now why would your husband . . . What? Your husband? Look, what's this apartment number?"

"309."

"309? Great Christ! I'm on the wrong floor! I live in 409. My key opened your door."

"Sit down, sweety," she said.

"No, no . . ."

I picked up the 4 remaining beers.

"Why rush right off?" she asked.

"Some men are crazy," I said, moving toward the door.

"What do you mean?"

"I mean, some men are in love with their wives."

She laughed. "Don't forget where I'm at."

I closed the door and walked up one more flight. Then I opened my door. There was nobody in there. The furniture was old and ripped, the rug almost colorless. Empty beer-cans on the floor. I was in the right place.

I took off my clothes, climbed into bed alone and cracked another beer.

# 7

WHILE WORKING DORSEY station I heard some of the old timers needling Big Daddy Greystone about how he'd had to buy a tape recorder in order to learn his schemes. Big Daddy had read the scheme sheet breaks onto the tape and listened to it as it played back. Big Daddy was called Big Daddy for obvious reasons. He'd put 3 women in the hospital with that thing. Now he'd found some roundeye. A fag named Carter. He'd even ripped Carter up. Carter had gone to a hospital in Boston. The joke was that Carter had to go all the way to Boston because there wasn't enough string on the West Coast to sew him up after Big

Daddy had finished with him. True or not, I decided to try the tape recorder. My worries were over. I could leave it on while I was sleeping. I had read somewhere that you could learn with your subconscious while sleeping. That seemed the easiest way out. I bought a machine and some tape.

I read the scheme sheet onto the tape, got into bed with my beer and listened:

"Now, HIGGINS BREAKS 42 HUNTER, 67 MARKLEY, 71 HUDSON, 84 EVERGLADES! AND NOW, LISTEN, LISTEN, CHINASKI, PITTSFIELD BREAKS 21 ASHGROVE, 33 SIMMONS, 46 NEEDLES! LISTEN, CHINASKI, LISTEN, WESTHAVEN BREAKS 11 EVERGREEN, 24 MARKHAM, 55 WOODTREE! CHINASKI, ATTENTION, CHINASKI! PARCHBLEAK BREAKS . . ."

It didn't work. My voice put me to sleep. I couldn't get past the 3rd beer.

After a while I didn't play the recorder or study the scheme sheet. I just drank my 6 tall cans of beer and went to sleep. I couldn't understand it. I even thought about going to see a psychiatrist. I envisioned the thing in my mind:

"Yes, my boy?"

"Well, it's like this."

"Go ahead. You need the couch?"

"No, thanks. I'd fall asleep."

"Go ahead, please."

"Well, I need my job."

"That's rational."

"But I have to study and pass 3 more schemes in order to keep it."

"Schemes? What are these 'schemes'?"

"That's when people don't put down zone numbers.

Somebody has to stick that letter. So we have to study these scheme sheets after working 12 hours a night."

"And?"

"I can't pick the sheet up. If I do, it falls from my hand."

"You can't study these schemes?"

"No. And I have to throw 100 cards in a glass cage in 8 minutes to at least an accuracy of 95 per cent or I'm out. And I need the job."

"Why can't you study these schemes?"

"That's why I'm here. To ask *you*. I must be crazy. But there are all those streets and they all break in different ways. Here look."

And I would hand him the 6 page scheme, stapled together at the top, small print on both sides.

He would flip through the pages.

"And you are supposed to memorize all this?"

"Yes, Doctor."

"Well, my boy," handing the sheets back, "you're not crazy for not wanting to study this. I'd be more apt to say that you were crazy if you *wanted* to study this. That'll be $25."

So I analyzed myself and kept the money.


BUT SOMETHING had to be done.

Then I had it. It was about 9:10 a.m. I phoned the Federal Building, Personnel Department.

"Miss Graves. I'd like to speak to Miss Graves, please."

"Hello?"

There she was. The bitch. I fondled myself as I spoke to her.

"Miss Graves. This is Chinaski. I filed an answer to your charge that I had a bad record. I don't know if you remember me?"

"We remember you, Mr. Chinaski."

"Has any decision been rendered?"

"Not yet. We'll let you know."

"All right, then. But I have a problem."

"Yes, Mr. Chinaski?"

"I am now studying the CP1." I paused.

"Yes?" she asked.

"I find it very difficult, I find it almost impossible to study this scheme, to put in all that extra time when it might be of no avail. I mean, I may be removed from the postal service at any moment. It is not fair to ask me to study the scheme under these conditions."

"All right, Mr. Chinaski. I'll phone the scheme room and instruct them to take you off the scheme until we have reached a decision."

"Thank you, Miss Graves."

"Good day," she said, and hung up.

It was a good day. And after fondling myself while on the phone I almost decided to go downstairs to 309. But I played it safe. I put on some bacon and eggs and celebrated with an extra quart of beer.

# 8

THEN THERE WERE only 6 or 7 of us. The CP1 was simply too much for the rest.

"How you doing on your scheme, Chinaski?" they asked me.

"No trouble at all," I said.

"O.K., break Woodburn Ave."

"Woodburn?"

"Yes, Woodburn."

"Listen, I don't like to be bothered with that stuff while I'm working. It bores me. One job at a time."

On Christmas I had Betty over. She baked a turkey and we drank. Betty always liked huge Christmas trees. It must have been 7 feet tall, and 1/2 as wide, covered with lights, bulbs, tinsel, various crap. We drank from a couple of fifths of whiskey, made love, ate our turkey, drank some more. The nail in the stand was loose and the stand was not big enough to hold the tree. I kept straightening it. Betty stretched out on the bed, passed out. I was drinking on the floor with my shorts on. Then I stretched out. Closed my eyes. Something awakened me. I opened my eyes. Just in time to see the huge tree covered with hot lights, leaning slowly toward me, the pointed star coming down like a dagger. I didn't quite know what it was. It looked like the end of the world. I couldn't move. The arms of the tree enfolded me. I was under it. The light bulbs were red hot.

"Oh, OH JESUS CHRIST, MERCY! LORD HELP ME! JESUS! JESUS! HELP!"

The bulbs were burning me. I rolled to the left, couldn't get out, then I rolled to the right.

"YAWK!"

I finally rolled out from under. Betty was up, standing there.

"What happened? What is it?"

"CAN'T YOU SEE? THAT GOD DAMNED TREE TRIED TO MURDER ME!"

"What?"

"YES, LOOK AT ME!"

I had red spots all over my body.

"Oh, *poor* baby!"

I walked over and pulled the plug from the wall. The lights went out. The thing was dead.

"Oh, my poor tree!"

"Your poor tree?"

"Yes, it was *so* pretty!"

"I'll stand it up in the morning. I don't trust it now. I'm giving it the rest of the night off."

She didn't like that. I could see an argument coming, so I stood the thing up behind a chair and turned the lights back on. If the thing had burned her tits or ass, she would have thrown it out the window. I thought I was being very kind.

SEVERAL DAYS after Christmas I stopped in to see Betty. She was sitting in her room, drunk, at 8:45 a.m. in the morning. She didn't look well but neither did I. It seemed that almost every roomer had given her a fifth. There was wine, vodka, whiskey, scotch. The cheapest brands. The bottles filled her room.

"Those damn fools! Don't they *know* any better? If you drink all this stuff it will kill you!"

Betty just looked at me. I saw it all in that look.

She had two children who never came to see her, never wrote her. She was a scrubwoman in a cheap hotel. When I had first met her her clothes had been expensive, trim ankles fitting into expensive shoes. She had been firm-fleshed, almost beautiful. Wild-eyed. Laughing. Coming from a rich husband, divorced from him, and he was to die in a car wreck, drunk, burning to death in Connecticut. "You'll never tame her," they told me.

There she was. But I'd had some help.

"Listen," I said, "I ought to take that stuff. I mean, I'll just give you back a bottle now and then. I won't drink it."

"Leave the bottles," Betty said. She didn't look at me. Her room was on the top floor and she sat in a chair by the window watching the morning traffic.

I walked over. "Look, I'm beat. I've got to leave. But for Christ's sake, take it easy on that stuff!"

87

"Sure," she said.

I leaned over and kissed her goodbye.

About a week and a half later I came by again. There wasn't any answer to my knock.

"Betty! Betty! Are you all right?"

I turned the knob. The door was open. The bed was turned back. There was a large bloodspot on the sheet.

"Oh shit!" I said. I looked around. All the bottles were gone.

Then I looked around. There was a middle-aged Frenchwoman who owned the place. She stood in the doorway.

"She's at County General Hospital. She was very sick. I called the ambulance last night."

"Did she drink all that stuff?"

"She had some help."

I ran down the stairway and got into my car. Then I was there. I knew the place well. They told me the room number.

There were 3 or 4 beds in a tiny room. A woman was sitting up in hers across the way, chewing an apple and laughing with two female visitors. I pulled the drop sheet around Betty's bed, sat down on the stool and leaned over her.

"Betty! Betty!"

I touched her arm.

"Betty!"

Her eyes opened. They were beautiful again. Bright calm blue.

"I knew it would be you," she said.

Then she closed her eyes. Her lips were parched. Yellow spittle had caked at the left corner of her mouth. I took a cloth and washed it away. I cleaned her face, hands and throat. I took another cloth and squeezed a bit of water on her tongue. Then a little more. I wet her lips. I straightened her hair. I heard the women laughing through the sheets that separated us.

"Betty, Betty, Betty. Please, I want you to drink some water, just a sip of water, not too much, just a sip."

She didn't respond. I tried for ten minutes. Nothing.

More spittle formed at her mouth. I wiped it away.

Then I got up and pulled the drop sheet back. I stared at the 3 women.

I walked out and spoke to the nurse at the desk. "Listen, why isn't anything being done for that woman in 45-c? Betty Williams."

"We're doing all we can, sir."

"But there's nobody there."

"We make our regular rounds."

"But where are the doctors? I don't see any doctors."

"The doctor has seen her, sir."

"Why do you just let her lay there?"

"We've done all we can, sir."

"SIR! SIR! SIR! FORGET THAT 'SIR' STUFF, WILL YOU? I'll bet if that were the president or governor or mayor or some rich son of a bitch, there would be doctors all over that room doing *something!* Why do you just let them die? What's the sin in being poor?"

"I've told you, sir, that we've done ALL we can."

"I'll be back in two hours."

"Are you her husband?"

"I used to be her common-law husband."

"May we have your name and phone number?"

I gave her that, then hurried out.

# 10

THE FUNERAL WAS to be at 10:30 a.m. but it was already hot. I had on a cheap black suit, bought and fitted in a rush. It was my first new suit in years. I had located the son. We drove along in his new Mercedes-Benz. I had traced him down with the help of a slip of paper with the address of his father-in-law on it. Two long distance calls and I had him. By the time he had driven in, his mother was dead. She died while I was making the phone calls. The kid, Larry, had never fit into the society thing. He had a habit of stealing cars from friends, but between the friends and the judge he managed to get off. Then the army got him, and somehow he got into a training program and when he got out he walked into a good-paying job. That's when he stopped seeing his mother, when he got that good job.

"Where's your sister?" I asked him.

"I don't know."

"This is a fine car. I can't even hear the engine."

Larry smiled. He liked that.

There were just 3 of us going to the funeral: son, lover and the subnormal sister of the owner of the hotel. Her name was Marcia. Marcia never said anything. She just sat around with this inane smile on her lips. Her skin was white as enamel. She had a mop of dead yellow hair and a hat that would not fit. Marcia had been sent by the owner in her place. The owner had to watch the hotel.

Of course, I had a very bad hangover. We stopped for coffee.

Already there had been trouble with the funeral. Larry had had an argument with the Catholic priest. There was some doubt that Betty was a true Catholic. The priest didn't want to do the service. Finally it was decided that he would do half a service. Well, half a service was better than none.

We even had trouble with the flowers. I had bought a wreath of roses, mixed roses, and they had been worked into a wreath. The flower shop spent an afternoon making it. The lady in the flower shop had known Betty. They had drank together a few years earlier when Betty and I had the house and dog. Delsie, her name was. I had always wanted to get into Delsie's pants but I never made it.

Delsie had phoned me. "Hank, what's the *matter* with those bastards?"

"Which bastards?"

"Those guys at the mortuary."

"What is it?"

"Well, I sent the boy in the truck to deliver your wreath and they didn't want to let him in. They said they were closed. You know, that's a long drive up there."

"Yeah, Delsie?"

"So finally they let the boy put the flowers inside the door but they wouldn't let him put them in the refrigerator. So the boy had to leave them inside the door. What the hell's wrong with those people?"

"I don't know. What the hell's wrong with people everywhere?"

"I won't be able to be at the funeral. Are you all right, Hank?"

"Why don't you come by and console me?"

"I'd have to bring Paul."

Paul was her husband.

"Forget it."

So there we were on our way to 1/2 a funeral.

Larry looked up from his coffee. "I'll write you about a headstone later. I don't have any more money now."

"All right," I said.

Larry paid for the coffees, then we went out and climbed into the Mercedes-Benz.

"Wait a minute," I said.

"What is it?" asked Larry.

"I think we forgot something."

I walked back into the cafe.

"Marcia."

She was still sitting at the table.

"We're leaving now, Marcia."

She got up and followed me out.

THE PRIEST read his thing. I didn't listen. There was the coffin. What had been Betty was in there. It was very hot. The sun came down in one yellow sheet. A fly circled around. Halfway through the halfway funeral two guys in working clothes came carrying my wreath. The roses were dead, dead and dying in the heat, and they leaned the thing up against a nearby tree. Near the end of the service my wreath leaned forward and fell flat on its face. Nobody picked it up. Then it was over. I walked up to the priest and shook his hand, "Thank you." He smiled. That made two smiling: the priest and Marcia.

On the way in, Larry said again:

"I'll write you about the headstone."

I'm still waiting for that letter.

# 11

I WENT UPSTAIRS to 409, had a stiff scotch and water, took some money out of the top drawer, went down the steps, got in my car and drove to the racetrack. I got there in time for the first race but didn't play it because I hadn't had time to read the form.

I went to the bar for a drink and I saw this high yellow walk by in an old raincoat. She was really dressed *down* but since I felt that way, I called her name just loud enough for her to hear as she walked by:

"Vi, baby."

She stopped, then came on over.

"Hi, Hank. How are you?"

I knew her from the central post office. She worked another station, the one near the water fountain, but she seemed more friendly than most.

"I've got the low blues. 3rd funeral in 2 years. First my mother, then my father. Today, an old girl friend."

She ordered something. I opened the Form.

"Let's catch this 2nd race."

She came over and leaned a lot of leg and breast against me. There was something under that raincoat. I always look for the non-public horse who could beat the favorite. If I found nobody could beat the favorite, I bet the favorite.

I had come to the racetrack after the other two funerals and had won. There was something about funerals. It made you see things better. A funeral a day and I'd be rich.

The 6 horse had lost by a neck to the favorite in a mile race last time out. The 6 had been overtaken by the favorite after a 2 length lead at the head of the stretch. The 6 had been 35/1. The favorite had been 9/2 in that race. Both were coming back in the same class. The favorite was adding two pounds, 116 to 118. The 6 still carried 116 but they had switched to a less popular jock, and also the distance was a mile and a 16th. The crowd figured that since the favorite had caught the 6 at a mile, then surely it would catch the 6 with the extra 16th of a mile to run. That seemed logical. But horse racing doesn't run to logic. Trainers enter their horses in what seems unfavorable conditions in order to keep the public money off the horse.

The distance switch, plus the switch to a less popular jock all pointed to a gallop at a good price. I looked at the board. The morning line was 5. The board read 7 to 1.

"It's the 6 horse," I told Vi.

"No, that horse is a quitter," she said.

"Yeah," I said, then walked over and put ten win on the 6.

The 6 took the lead out of the gate, hugged the rail around the first turn, then under an easy hold kept a length and a quarter lead down the backstretch. The pack followed. They figured the 6 would lead around the curve, then open up at the top of the stretch, and then they'd go after it. That was standard procedure. But the trainer had given the boy different instructions. At the top of the curve the boy let out the string and the horse leaped forward. Before the other jocks could get to their mounts, the 6 had a 4 length lead. At the top of the stretch the boy gave the 6 a slight breather, looked back, then let it out again. I was looking good. Then the favorite, 9/5, came out of the pack and the son of a bitch was moving. It was eating up the lengths, driving. It looked like it was going to drive right past my horse. The favorite was the 2 horse. Halfway down the stretch, the 2 was a half length behind the 6, then the boy on the 6 went to the whip. The boy on the favorite *had* been whipping. They went the rest of the stretch that way, a half length apart, and that's what it was at the wire. I looked at the board. My horse had risen to 8 to 1.

We walked back to the bar.

"The best horse didn't win that race," said Vi.

"I don't care who's best. All I want is the front number. Order up."

We ordered.

"All right, smart boy. Let's see you get the next one."

"I tell you, baby, I am hell coming out of funerals."

She put that leg and breast up against me. I took a nip of scotch and opened the Form. 3rd race.

I looked it over. They were out to murder the crowd that day. The early foot had just won, so now the crowd was conscious of the speed horse and down on the stretch runners. The crowd only goes back one race in their memory. Part of it is caused by the 25 minutes wait between races. All they can think of is what had just happened.

The 3rd race was 6 furlongs. Now the speed horse, the early foot was the favorite. It had lost its last race by a nose at 7 furlongs, holding the lead all the way down the stretch and losing in the last jump. The 8 horse was the closer. It had finished 3rd, a length and a half behind the favorite, closing 2 lengths in the stretch. The crowd figured that if the 8 hadn't caught the favorite at 7 furlongs, how in the hell could he catch it with a furlong less to go? The crowd always went home broke. The horse who had won the 7 furlong race wasn't in today's race.

"It's the 8 horse," I told Vi.

"The distance is too short. He'll never get up," said Vi.

The 8 horse was 6 on the line and read 9.

I collected from the last race, then put a ten win on the 8 horse. If you bet too heavy your horse loses. Or you change your mind and get off your horse. Ten win was a nice comfortable bet.

The favorite looked good. It came out of the gate first, got the rail and opened up two lengths. The 8 was running wide, next to last, gradually moving in closer to the rail. The favorite still looked good at the top of the stretch. The boy took the 8 horse, now running 5th, wide, gave it a taste of the whip. Then the favorite began to shorten stride. It had gone the first quarter in 22 and 4/5, but it

95

still had 2 lengths halfway down the stretch. Then the 8 horse just blew by, breezing, and won by 2 and 1/2 lengths. I looked at the board. It still read 9 to 1.

We went back to the bar. Vi really laid her body against me.

I won 3 of the last 5 races. They only ran 8 races in those days instead of 9. Anyhow, 8 races was enough that day. I bought a couple of cigars and we got into my car. Vi had come out on the bus. I stopped for a 5th, then we went up to my place.

# 12

VI LOOKED AROUND.

"What's a guy like you doing in a place like this?"

"That's what all the girls ask me."

"It's really a rat hole."

"It keeps me modest."

"Let's go to my place."

"O.k."

We got into my car and she told me where she lived. We stopped for a couple of big steaks, vegetables, stuff for a salad, potatoes, bread, more to drink.

In the hallway of her apartment house there was a sign:

NO LOUD NOISE OR DISTURBANCE
OF ANY KIND ALLOWED. TV SETS
MUST BE OFF AT 10 P.M.
WE HAVE WORKING PEOPLE HERE.

It was a large sign done up in red paint.

"I like that part about the t.v. sets," I told her.

We took the elevator up. She did have a nice place. I

carried the bags into the kitchen, found two glasses, poured two drinks.

"You get the stuff out. I'll be right back."

I pulled the stuff out, laid it on the sink. Had another drink. Vi came back. She was all dressed. Ear rings, high heels, short skirt. She looked all right. Stocky. But good ass and thighs, breasts. A hard tough ride.

"Hello there," I said, "I'm a friend of Vi's. She said she'd be right back. Care for a drink?"

She laughed, then I grabbed that big body and gave her a kiss. Her lips were cold as diamonds but tasted good.

"I'm hungry," she said. "Let me cook!"

"I'm hungry too. I'll eat *you!*"

She laughed. I gave her a short kiss, grabbing her ass. Then I walked into the front room with my drink, sat down, stretched my legs, sighed.

I could stay here, I thought, make money at the track while she nurses me over the bad moments, rubs oils on my body, cooks for me, talks to me, goes to bed with me. Of course, there would always be arguments. That is the nature of Woman. They like the mutual exchange of dirty laundry, a bit of screaming, a bit of dramatics. Then an exchange of vows. I wasn't very good on the exchange of vows.

I was getting high. In my mind I'd already moved in.

Vi had everything going. She came out with her drink, sat on my lap, kissed me, putting her tongue into my mouth My cock leaped up against her firm bottom. I grabbed a handful. Squeezed.

"I want to show you something," she said.

"I know you do but let's wait until about an hour after dinner."

"Oh, I don't mean that!"

I reached for her and gave her the tongue.

Vi got off my lap.

"No, I want to show you a photo of my daughter. She's in Detroit with my mother. But she's coming out here in the Fall to go to school."

"How old is she?"

"6."

"And the father?"

"I divorced Roy. The son of a bitch was no good. All he did was drink and play the horses."

"Oh?"

She came back with the photo, put it in my hand. I tried to make it out. There was a dark background.

"Listen, Vi, she's really *black!* God damn, don't you have sense enough to take this with a light background?"

"It's from her father. The black dominates."

"Yeh. I can see that."

"My mother took the photo."

"I'm sure you have a nice daughter."

"Yes, she is nice, really."

Vi put the photo back and went into the kitchen.

The eternal photo! Women with their photos. It was the same over and over and over again. Vi stood in the kitchen doorway.

"Don't drink too much now! You know what we have to do!"

"Don't worry, baby, I'll have something for you. Meanwhile, bring me a drink! I've had a hard day. Half scotch, half water."

"Get your own drink, bigshot."

I turned my chair around, flicked on the t.v.

"You want another good day at the track, woman, you better bring Mr. Bigshot a drink. And I mean now!"

Vi had finally bet my horse in the last race. It was a 5/1 shot who hadn't shown a decent race in 2 years. I bet it merely because it was 5/1 when it should have been 20. The horse had won by 6 lengths, eased up. They had that baby fixed from asshole to nostril.

I looked up and here was a hand with a drink reaching over my shoulder.

"Thanks, baby."

"Yes, master," she laughed.

# 13

IN BED I had something in front of me but I couldn't do anything with it. I whaled and I whaled and I whaled. Vi was very patient. I kept striving and banging but I'd had too much to drink.

"Sorry, baby," I said. Then I rolled off. And went to sleep.

Then something awakened me. It was Vi. She had stoked me up and was riding topside.

"Go, baby, go!" I told her.

I arched my back now and then. She looked down at me with little greedy eyes. I was being raped by a high yellow enchantress! For a moment, it excited me.

Then I told her. "Shit. Get down, baby. It's been a long hard day. There will be a better time."

She climbed off. The thing went down like an express elevator.

# 14

IN THE MORNING I heard her walking around. She walked and she walked and she walked.

It was about 10:30 a.m. I was sick. I didn't want to face her. 15 more minutes. Then I'd get out.

She shook me. "Listen, I want you to get out of here before my girlfriend shows!"

"So what? I'll screw her too."

"Yeah," she laughed, "yeah."

I got up. Coughed, gagged. Slowly got into my clothes.

"You make me feel like a wash-out," I told her. "I *can't* be that bad! There must be *some* good in me."

I finally got dressed. I went to the bathroom and threw some water on my face, combed my hair. If I could only comb that face, I thought, but I can't.

I came out.

"Vi."

"Yes?"

"Don't be too pissed. It wasn't you. It was the booze. It has happened before."

"All right, then, you shouldn't drink so much. No woman likes to come in second to a bottle."

"Why don't you bet me to place then?"

"Oh, stop it!"

"Listen, you need any money, babe?"

I reached into my wallet and took out a twenty. I handed it to her.

"My, you *are* sweet!"

Her hand touched my cheek, she kissed me gently along the side of the mouth.

"Drive carefully now."

"Sure, babe."

I drove carefully all the way to the racetrack.

# 15

THEY HAD ME in the counselor's office in one of the back rooms of the second floor.

"Let me see how you look, Chinaski."

He looked at me.

"Ow! You look bad. I better take a pill."

Sure enough, he opened a bottle and took one.

"All right, Mr. Chinaski, we'd like to know where you've been the last two days?"

"Mourning."

"Mourning? Mourning about what?"

"Funeral. Old friend. One day to pack in the stiff. One day to mourn."

"But you didn't phone in, Mr. Chinaski."

"Yeh."

"And I want to tell you something, Chinaski, off the record."

"All right."

"When you don't phone in, you know what you are saying?"

"No."

"Mr. Chinaski, you are saying, 'Fuck the post office!'"

"I am?"

"And, Mr. Chinaski, you know what that means?"

"No, what does it mean?"

"That means, Mr. Chinaski, that the post office is going to fuck *you!*"

Then he leaned back and looked at me.

"Mr. Feathers," I told him, "you can go to hell."

"Don't get fresh, Henry. I can make it tough on you."

"Please address me by my full name, sir. I ask for a simple bit of respect from you."

"You ask respect for me but . . ."

"That's right. We know where you park, Mr. Feathers."

"What? Is that a threat?"

"The blacks love me here, Feathers. I have fooled them."

"The blacks love you?"

"They give me water. I even fuck their women. Or try to."

"All right. This is getting out of hand. Please report back to your assignment."

He handed me my travel slip. He was worried, poor fellow. I hadn't fooled the blacks. I hadn't fooled anybody but Feathers. But you couldn't blame him for worrying. One supervisor had been pushed down the stairway. Another slashed across the ass. Another knifed in the belly as he was waiting in the crosswalk for the signal to change at 3 a.m. Right in front of the central post office. We never saw him again.

Feathers, soon after I spoke to him, bid out of the central office, I don't know exactly where he went. But it was out of the central office.

# 16

ONE MORNING ABOUT 10 a.m. the phone rang. "Mr. Chinaski?"

I recognised the voice and began to fondle myself.

"Ummmm," I said.

It was Miss Graves, that bitch.

"Were you asleep?"

"Yes, yes, Miss Graves, but go on. It's all right, it's all right."

"Well, you've made clearance."

"Ummm, ummm."

"So therefore we have notified the scheme room."

"Ummhmm."

"And you are scheduled to throw your CP1 two weeks from today."

"What? Now wait a minute . . ."
"That's all, Mr. Chinaski. Good day."
She hung up.

# 17

WELL, I TOOK the scheme sheet and I related everything to
sex and age. This guy lived in this house with 3 women.
He beltwhipped one (her name was the name of the street
and her age the break number); he ate another (ditto), and
he simply screwed the third old-fashioned (ditto). There
were all these fags and one of them (his name was Manfred
Ave.) was 33 years old . . . etc., etc., etc.

I'm sure they wouldn't have let me into that glass cage
if they had known what I was thinking as I looked at all
those cards. They all looked like old friends to me.

Still, I got some of my orgies crossed. I threw a 94 the
first time.

Ten days later, when I came back, I knew who was doing
what to whom.

I threw 100 per cent in 5 minutes.

And got a form letter of congratulation from the City
Postmaster.

# 18

SOON AFTER THAT I made regular and that gave me an 8
hour night, which beat 12, and pay for holidays. Of the 150
or 200 that had come in, there were only two of us left.

Then I met David Janko on the station. He was a young
white in his early twenties. I made the mistake of talking
to him, something about classical music. I happened to be
up on my classical music because it was the only thing I

could listen to while drinking beer in bed in the early morning. If you listen morning after morning you are bound to remember things. And when Joyce had divorced me I had mistakenly packed 2 volumes of *The Lives of the Classical and Modern Composers* into one of my suitcases. Most of these men's lives were so tortured that I enjoyed reading about them, thinking, well, I am in hell too and I can't even write music.

But I had opened my mouth. Janko and some other guy were arguing and I settled it by giving them Beethoven's birthdate, when he had penned the 3rd Symphony, and a generalized (if confused) idea of what the critics said about the 3rd.

It was too much for Janko. He immediately mistook me for a learned man. Sitting on the stool next to me he began to complain and rant, night after long night, about the misery buried deep in his twisted and pissed soul. He had a terribly loud voice and he wanted everybody to hear. I flipped the letters in, I listened and listened and listened, thinking what will I do now? How will I get this poor mad bastard to shut up?

I went home each night dizzy and sick. He was murdering me with the sound of his voice.

# 19

I BEGAN AT 6:18 p.m. and Dave Janko did not begin until 10:36 p.m., so it could have been worse. Having a 10.06 thirty minute lunch, I was usually back by the time he got in. In he'd come, looking for a stool next to mine. Janko, besides playing at the great mind also played at the great lover. According to him, he was trapped in hallways by beautiful young women, followed down the streets by them. They wouldn't let him rest, poor fellow. But I never saw him speak to a woman down at work, nor did they to him.

In he'd come: "HEY, HANK! MAN, I REALLY CAUGHT A HEAD JOB TODAY!"

He didn't speak, he screamed. He screamed all night.

"JESUS CHRIST, SHE REALLY ATE ME UP! AND YOUNG TOO! BUT SHE WAS REALLY A PRO!"

I lit a cigarette.

Then I had to hear all about how he met her—

"I HAD TO GO OUT FOR A LOAF OF BREAD, SEE?"

Then—down to the last detail—what she said, what he said, what they did, etc.

At that time, a law was passed requiring the post office to pay substitute clerks time and one half. So the post office shifted the overtime to the regular clerks.

Eight or ten minutes before my regular quitting time of 2:48 a.m. the intercom would come on:

"Your attention, please! All regular clerks who reported at 6:18 p.m., are required to work one hour overtime!"

Janko would smile, lean forward and pour more of his poison into me.

Then, 8 minutes before my 9th hour was up, the intercom would come on again.

"Your attention, please! All regular clerks who reported at 6:18 p.m., are required to work two hours overtime!"

Then 8 minutes before my 10th hour:

"Your attention, please! All regular clerks who reported at 6:18 p.m., are required to work 3 hours overtime!"

Meanwhile Janko never stopped.

"I WAS SITTING IN THIS DRUGSTORE, YOU SEE. TWO CLASS BROADS CAME IN. ONE OF THEM SAT ON EACH SIDE OF ME . . ."

The boy was murdering me but I couldn't find any way out. I remembered all the other jobs I had worked at. I had drawn the nut each time. They liked me.

Then Janko put his novel on me. He couldn't type and had the thing typed up by a professional. It was enclosed in a fancy black leather notebook. The title was very romantic. "LET ME KNOW WHAT YOU THINK ABOUT IT," he said.

"Yeh," I said.

# 20

I TOOK IT home, opened the beer, got into bed and began.

It started well. It was about how Janko had lived in small rooms and starved while trying to find a job. He had trouble with the employment agencies. And there was a guy he met in a bar—he seemed like a very learned type—but his friend kept borrowing money from him which he never paid back.

It was honest writing.

Maybe I have misjudged this man, I thought.

I was hoping for him as I read. Then the novel fell apart. For some reason the moment he started writing about the post office, the thing lost reality.

The novel got worse and worse. It ended up with him being at the opera. It was intermission. He had left his seat in order to get away from the coarse and stupid crowd. Well, I was with him there. Then, rounding a pillar, it happened. It happened very quickly. He crashed into this cultured, dainty, beautiful thing. Almost knocked her down.

The dialogue went like this:

"Oh, I'm *so* sorry!"

"It's quite all right . . ."

"I didn't mean to . . . you know . . . I'm sorry . . ."

"Oh, I assure you, it's all right!"

"But I mean, I didn't see you . . . I didn't mean to . . ."

"It's all right. It's quite all right . . ."

The dialogue about the bumping went on for a page and a half.

The poor boy was truly mad.

It turned out this broad, although she's wandering around among the pillars alone, well, she's really married to this doctor, but the doc didn't comprehend opera, or for that matter, didn't even care for such simple things as Ravel's *Bolero*. Or even *The Three-Cornered Hat Dance* by de Falla. I was with the doc there.

From the bumping of these two true sensitive souls, something developed. They met at concerts and had a quickie afterwards. (This was *inferred* rather than stated, for both of them were too delicate to simply *fuck*.)

Well, it ended. The poor beautiful creature loved her husband and she loved the hero (Janko). She didn't know what to do, so, of course, she committed suicide. She left both the doc and Janko standing in their bathrooms alone.

I TOLD the kid, "It starts well. But you'll have to take out that bumping-around-the-pillar dialogue. It's very bad . . ."

"No!" he said. "EVERYTHING STAYS!"

THE MONTHS went by and the novel kept coming back.

"JESUS CHRIST!" he said, "I CAN'T GO TO NEW YORK AND SHAKE THE HANDS OF THE PUB-LISHERS!"

"Look, kid, why don't you quit this job? Go to a small room and write. Work it out."

"A GUY LIKE YOU CAN DO THAT," he said, "BECAUSE YOU LOOK LIKE A WINO. PEOPLE WILL HIRE YOU BECAUSE THEY FIGURE YOU CAN'T GET A JOB ANYWHERE ELSE AND YOU'LL STAY. THEY WON'T HIRE ME BECAUSE THEY LOOK AT ME AND THEY SEE HOW INTELLIGENT I AM AND THEY THINK, WELL, AN INTELLIGENT MAN LIKE HIM WON'T STAY WITH US, SO THERE'S NO USE HIRING HIM."

"I still say, go to a small room and write."

"BUT I NEED ASSURANCE!"

"It's a good thing a few others didn't think that way. It's a good thing Van Gogh didn't think that way."

"VAN GOGH'S BROTHER GAVE HIM FREE PAINTS!" the kid said to me.

# IV

## 1

THEN I DEVELOPED a new system at the racetrack. I pulled in $3,000 in a month and a half while only going to the track two or three times a week. I began to dream. I saw a little house down by the sea. I saw myself in fine clothing, calm, getting up mornings, getting into my imported car, making the slow easy drive to the track. I saw leisurely steak dinners, preceded and followed by good chilled drinks in colored glasses. The big tip. The cigar. And women as you wanted them. It's easy to fall into this kind of thinking when men handed you large bills at the cashier's window. When in one six furlong race, say in a minute and 9 seconds, you make a month's pay.

So I stood in the tour superintendent's office. There he was behind his desk. I had a cigar in my mouth and whiskey on my breath. I felt like money. I looked like money.

"Mr. Winters," I said, "the post office has treated me. well. But I have outside business interests that simply must be taken care of. If you can't give me a leave of absence, I must resign."

"Didn't I give you a leave of absence earlier in the year, Chinaski?"

"No, Mr. Winters, you turned down my request for a leave of absence. This time there can't be any turndown. Or I will resign."

"All right, fill out the form and I'll sign it. But I can only give you 90 working days off."

"I'll take 'em." I said, exhaling a long trail of blue smoke from my expensive cigar.

# 2

THE TRACK HAD moved down the coast a hundred miles or so. I kept paying the rent on my apartment in town, got in my car and drove down. Once or twice a week I would drive back to the apartment, check the mail, maybe sleep overnight, then drive back down.

It was a good life, and I started winning. After the last race each night I would have one or two easy drinks at the bar, tipping the bartender well. It looked like a new life. I could do no wrong.

One night I didn't even watch the last race. I went to the bar.

$50 to win was my standard bet. After you bet 50 win a while it feels like betting 5 win or 10 win.

"Scotch and water," I told the barkeep. "Think I'll listen to this one over the speaker."

"Who you got?"

"Blue Stocking," I told him. "50 win."

"Too much weight."

"Are you kidding? A good horse can pack 122 pounds in a 6 thousand dollar claimer. That means, according to the conditions, that the horse has done something that no other horse in that race has done."

Of course, that wasn't the reason I had bet Blue

Stocking. I was always giving out misinformation. I didn't want anybody else on board.

At the time, they didn't have closed circuit t.v. You just listened to the calls. I was $380 ahead. A loss on the last race would give me a $330 profit. A good day's work.

We listened. The caller mentioned every horse in the race but Blue Stocking.

My horse must have fallen down, I thought.

They were in the stretch, coming down toward the wire. That track was notorious for its short stretch.

Then right before the race ended the announcer screamed, "AND HERE COMES BLUE STOCKING ON THE OUTSIDE! BLUE STOCKING IS GETTING UP! IT'S . . . BLUE STOCKING!"

"Pardon me," I told the bartender, "I'll be right back. Fix me a scotch and water, double shot."

"Yes, sir!" he said.

I went out back where they had a small tote board near the walking ring. Blue Stocking read 9/2. Well it wasn't 8 or 10 to one. But you played the winner, not the price. I'd take the $250 profit plus change. I went back to the bar.

"Who do you like tomorrow, sir?" asked the barkeep.

"Tomorrow's a long way off," I told him.

I finished my drink, tipped him a dollar and walked off.

# 3

EVERY NIGHT WAS about the same. I'd drive along the coast looking for a place to have dinner. I wanted an expensive place that wasn't too crowded. I developed a nose for those places. I could tell by looking at them from the outside. You couldn't always get a table directly overlooking the ocean unless you wanted to wait. But you could still see the ocean out there and the moon, and let yourself get romantic. Let yourself enjoy life. I always asked for a small salad and a big steak. The waitresses smiled deliciously and stood very close to you. I had come a long way from a guy who had worked in slaughterhouses, who had crossed the country with a railroad track gang, who had worked in a dog biscuit factory, who had slept on park benches, who had worked the nickel and dime jobs in a dozen cities across the nation.

After dinner I would look for a motel. This also took a bit of driving. First I'd stop somewhere for whiskey and beer. I avoided the places with t.v. sets. It was clean sheets, a hot shower, luxury. It was a magic life. And I did not tire of it.

# 4

ONE DAY I was at the bar between races and I saw this woman. God or somebody keeps creating women and tossing them out on the streets, and this one's ass is too big and that one's tits are too small and this one is mad and that one is crazy and that one is a religionist and that one reads tea leaves and this one can't control her farts, and that one has this big nose, and that one has boney legs
. . .

But now and then, a woman walks up, full blossom, a woman just bursting out of her dress . . . a sex creature, a curse, the end of it all. I looked up and there she was, down at the end of the bar. She was about drunk and the bartender wouldn't serve her and she began to bitch and they called one of the track cops and the track cop had her by the arm, leading her off, and they were talking.

I finished my drink and followed them.

"Officer! Officer!"

He stopped and looked at me.

"Has my wife done something wrong?" I asked.

"We believe that she is intoxicated, sir. I was going to escort her to the gate."

"The starting gate?"

He laughed. "No, sir. The exit gate."

"I'll take over here, officer."

"All right, sir. But see that she doesn't drink anymore."

I didn't answer. I took her by the arm and led her back in.

"Thank god, you saved my life," she said.

Her flank bumped against me.

"It's all right. My name's Hank."

"I'm Mary Lou," she said.

"Mary Lou," I said, "I love you."

She laughed.

"By the way, you don't hide behind pillars at the opera house, do you?"

"I don't hide behind anything," she said, sticking her breasts out.

"Want another drink?"

"Sure, but he won't serve me."

"There's more than one bar at this track, Mary Lou. Let's take a run upstairs. And keep quiet. Stand back and I will bring your drink to you. What're you drinking?"

"Anything," she said.

"Scotch and water do?"

"Sure."

We drank the rest of the card. She brought me luck. I hit two of the last three.

"Did you bring a car?" I asked her.

"I came with some damn fool," she said. "Forget him."

"If you can, I can," I told her.

We wrapped up in the car and her tongue flicked in and out of my mouth like a tiny lost snake. We unwrapped and I drove down the coast. It was a lucky night. I got a table overlooking the ocean and we ordered drinks and waited for the steaks. Everybody in the place looked at her. I leaned forward and lit her cigarette, thinking, this one's going to be a good one. Everybody in the place knew what I was thinking and Mary Lou knew what I was thinking, and I smiled at her over the flame.

"The ocean," I said, "look at it out there, battering, crawling up and down. And underneath all that, the fish, the poor fish fighting each other, eating each other. We're like those fish, only we're up here. One bad move and you're finished. It's nice to be a champion. It's nice to know your moves."

I took out a cigar and lit it.

" 'nother drink, Mary Lou?"

"All right, Hank."

# 5

THERE WAS THIS place. It stretched over the sea, it was built over the sea. An odd place, but with a touch of class. We got a room on the first floor. You could hear the ocean running down there, you could hear the waves, you could *smell* the ocean, you could feel the tide going in and out, in and out.

I took my time with her as we talked and drank. Then I went over to the couch and sat next to her. We worked something up, laughing and talking and listening to the ocean. I stripped down but made her keep her clothes on. Then I carried her over to the bed and while crawling all over her, I finally worked her clothing off and I was in. It was hard getting in. Then she gave way.

It was one of the best. I heard the water, I heard the tide going in and out. It was as if I were coming with the whole ocean. It seemed to last and last. Then I rolled off.

"Oh Jesus Christ," I said, "Oh Jesus Christ!"

I don't know how Jesus Christ always got into such things.

# 6

THE NEXT DAY we picked up some of her stuff at this motel. There was a little dark guy in there with a wart on the side of his nose. He looked dangerous.

"You going with him?" he asked Mary Lou.

"Yes."

"All right. Luck." He lit a cigarette.

"Thanks, Hector."

Hector? What the hell kind of name was that?

"Care for a beer?" he asked me.

"Sure," I said.

Hector was sitting on the edge of the bed. He went into the kitchen and got three beers. It was good beer, imported from Germany. He opened Mary Lou's bottle, poured some of the bottle into a glass for her. Then he asked me:

"Glass?"

"No, thanks."

I got up and switched bottles with him.

We sat drinking the beer in silence.

Then he said, "You're man enough to take her away from me?"

"Hell, I don't know. It's her choice. If she wants to stay with you, she'll stay. Why don't you ask her?"

"Mary Lou, will you stay with me?"

"No," she said, "I'm going with him."

She pointed at me. I felt important. I had lost so many women to so many other guys that it felt good for the thing to be working the other way around. I lit a cigar. Then I looked around for an ashtray. I saw one on the dresser.

I happened to look into the mirror to see how hungover I was and I saw him coming at me like a dart toward a dartboard. I still had the beerbottle in my hand. I swung and he walked right into it. I got him in the mouth. His whole mouth was broken teeth and blood. Hector dropped to his knees, crying, holding his mouth with both hands. I saw the stiletto. I kicked the stiletto away from him with my foot, picked it up, looked at it. 9 inches. I hit the button and the blade dropped back in. I put the thing in my pocket.

Then as Hector was crying I walked up and booted him in the ass. He sprawled flat on the floor, still crying. I walked over, took a pull at his beer.

Then I walked over and slapped Mary Lou. She screamed.

"Cunt! You set this up, didn't you? You'd let this monkey kill me for the lousy 4 or 5 hundred bucks in my wallet!"

"No, no!" she said. She was crying. They both were crying.

I slapped her again.

"Is that how you make it, cunt? Killing men for a couple of hundred?"

"No, no, I LOVE you, Hank, I LOVE you!"

I grabbed that blue dress by the neck and ripped one side of it down to her waist. She didn't wear a brassiere. The bitch didn't need one.

I walked out of there, got outside and drove toward the track. For two or three weeks I was looking over my shoulder. I was jumpy. Nothing happened. I never saw Mary Lou at the racetrack again. Or Hector.

# 7

SOMEHOW THE MONEY slipped away after that and soon I left the track and sat around in my apartment waiting for the 90 days' leave to run out. My nerves were raw from the drinking and the action. It's not a new story about how women descend upon a man. You think you have space to breathe, then you look up and there's another one. A few days after returning to work, there was another one. Fay. Fay had grey hair and always dressed in black. She said she was protesting the war. But if Fay wanted to protest the war, that was all right with me. She was a writer of some sort and went to a couple of writers' workshops. She had ideas about Saving the World. If she could Save it for me, that would be all right too. She had been living off alimony checks from a former husband—they had had 3 children—and her mother also sent money now and then. Fay had not had more than one or two jobs in her life.

Meanwhile Janko had a new load of bullshit. He sent me home each morning with my head aching. At the time I was getting numerous traffic citations. It seemed that everytime I looked into the rear view mirror there were the red lights. A squad car or a bike.

I got to my place late one night. I was really beat. Getting that key out and into the door was about the last of me. I walked into the bedroom and there was Fay in bed reading the *New Yorker* and eating chocolates. She didn't even say hello.

I walked into the kitchen and looked for something to eat. There was nothing in the refrigerator. I decided to pour myself a glass of water. I walked to the sink. It was stopped-up with garbage. Fay liked to save empty jars and jar lids. The dirty dishes filled half the sink and on top of the water, along with a few paper plates, floated these jars and jar lids.

I walked back into the bedroom just as Fay was putting a chocolate in her mouth.

"Look, Fay," I said, "I know you want to save the world. But can't you start in the kitchen?"

"Kitchens aren't important," she said.

It was difficult to hit a woman with grey hair so I just went into the bathroom and let the water run into the tub. A burning bath might cool the nerves. When the tub was full I was afraid to get into it. My sore body had, by then, stiffened to such an extent that I was afraid I might drown in there.

I went into the front room and after an effort I managed to get out of my shirt, pants, shoes, stockings. I walked into the bedroom and climbed into bed next to Fay. I couldn't get settled. Every time I moved, it cost me.

The only time you are alone, Chinaski, I thought, is when you are driving to work or driving back.

I finally worked my way to a position on my stomach. I ached all over. Soon I'd be back on the job. If I could manage to sleep, it would help. Every now and then I could hear a page turn, the sound of chocolates being eaten. It had been one of her writers' workshop nights. If she would only turn out the lights.

"How was the workshop?" I asked from my belly.

"I'm worried about Robby."

"Oh," I asked, "what's wrong?"

Robby was a guy nearing forty who had lived with his mother all his life. All he wrote, I was told, were terribly funny stories about the Catholic Church. Robby really laid it to the Catholics. The magazines just weren't ready for Robby, although he had been printed once in a Canadian journal. I had seen Robby once on one of my nights off. I drove Fay up to this mansion where they all read their stuff to each other. "Oh! There's Robby!" Fay had said, "he writes these very funny stories about the Catholic Church!"

She had pointed. Robby had his back to us. His ass was wide and big and soft; it hung in his slacks. Can't they see that? I thought.

"Won't you come in?" Fay had asked.

"Maybe next week . . ."

FAY PUT another chocolate into her mouth.

"Robby's worried. He lost his job on the delivery truck. He says he can't write without a job. He needs a feeling of security. He says he won't be able to write until he finds another job."

"Oh hell," I said, "I can get him another job."

"Where? How?"

"They are hiring down at the post office, right and left. The pay's not bad."

"THE POST OFFICE! ROBBY'S TOO SENSITIVE TO WORK AT THE POST OFFICE!"

"Sorry," I said, "thought it was worth a try. Good night."

Fay didn't answer me. She was angry.

# 8

I HAD FRIDAYS and Saturdays off, which made Sunday the roughest day. Plus the fact that on Sunday they made me report at 3:30 p.m. instead of my usual 6:18 p.m.

This Sunday I went in and they put me in the station papers section, as usual per Sundays, and this meant at *least* eight hours on my feet.

Besides the pains, I was beginning to suffer from dizzy spells. Everything would whirl, I would come very close to blacking out, then I would grab myself.

It had been a brutal Sunday. Some friends of Fay's had come over and sat on the couch and chirped, how they were really great writers, really the best in the nation. The only reason they didn't get published was that they didn't—they said—send their stuff out.

I had looked at them. If they wrote the way they looked, drinking their coffee and giggling and dipping their doughnuts, it didn't matter if they sent it or jammed it.

I was sticking in the magazines this Sunday. I needed coffee, 2 coffees, a bite to eat. But all the soups were standing out front. I hit out the back way. I had to get straight. The cafeteria was on the 2nd floor. I was on the 4th. There was doorway down by the men's crapper. I looked at the sign.

## WARNING!
## DO NOT USE THIS
## STAIRWAY!

It was a con. I was wiser than those mothers. They just put the sign up to keep clever guys like Chinaski from going down to the cafeteria. I opened the door and went on down. The door closed behind me. I walked down the second floor. Turned the knob. What the fuck! The door wouldn't open! It was locked. I walked back up. Past the 3rd floor door. I didn't try it. I knew it was locked. As the first floor was locked. I knew the post office well enough by then. When they laid a trap, they were thorough. I had one slim chance. I was at the 4th floor. I tried the knob. It was locked.

At least the door was near the men's crapper. There was always somebody going in an out of the men's crapper. I waited. 10 minutes. 15 minutes. 20 minutes! Didn't ANYBODY want to shit, piss or goof-off? 25 minutes. Then I saw a face. I tapped on the glass.

"Hey, buddy! HEY, BUDDY!"

He didn't hear me, or he pretended not to hear me. He marched into the crapper. 5 minutes. Then another face came by.

I rapped hard. "HEY, BUDDY! HEY. YOU COCK-SUCKER!"

I guess he heard me. He looked at me from behind the wired glass.

I said, "OPEN THE DOOR! CAN'T YOU SEE ME IN HERE? I'M LOCKED IN, YOU FOOL! OPEN THE DOOR!"

He opened the door. I went in. The guy was in a trance-like state.

I squeezed his elbow.

"Thanks, kid."

I walked back to the magazine case.

Then the soup walked past. He stopped and looked at me. I slowed down.

"How are you doing, Mr. Chinaski?"

I growled at him, waved a magazine in the air as if I were going insane, said something to myself, and he walked on.

## 9

FAY WAS PREGNANT. But it didn't change her and it didn't change the post office either.

The same clerks did all the work while the miscellaneous crew stood around and argued about sports. They were all big black dudes—built like professional wrestlers. Whenever a new one came into the service he was tossed into the miscellaneous crew. This kept them from murdering the supervisors. If the miscellaneous crew had a supervisor you never saw him. The crew brought in truckloads of mail that arrived via freight elevator. This was a 5 minute on the hour job. Sometimes they counted the mail, or pretended to. They looked very calm and intellectual, making their counts with long pencils behind one ear. But most of the time they argued the sports scene violently. They were all experts—they read the same sports writers.

"All right, man, what's your all time outfield?"

"Well, Willie Mays, Ted Williams, Cobb."

"What? What?"

"That's right, baby!"

"What about the Babe? Whatta ya gonna do with the Babe?"

"O.K., O.K., who's your all star outfield?"

"All time, not all star!"

"O.K., O.K., you know what I mean, baby, you know what I mean!"

"Well, I'll take Mays, Ruth and Di Maj!"

"Both you guys are nuts! How about Hank Aaron, Baby? How about Hank?"

At one time, all miscellaneous jobs were put on bid. Bids were filled mostly on the basis of seniority. The miscellaneous crew went about and ripped the bids out of the order books. Then they had nothing to do. Nobody filed a complaint. It was a long dark walk to the parking lot at night.

# 10

I BEGAN GETTING dizzy spells. I could feel them coming. The case would begin to whirl. The spells lasted about a minute. I couldn't understand it. Each letter was getting heavier and heavier. The clerks began to have that dead grey look. I began to slide off my stool. My legs would barely hold me up. The job was killing me.

I went to the doctor and told him about it. He took my blood pressure.

"No, no, your blood pressure is all right."

Then he put the stethoscope to me and weighed me.

"I can find nothing wrong."

Then he gave me a special blood test. He took blood from my arm three times at intervals, each time lapse longer than the last.

"Do you care to wait in the other room?"

"No, no, I'll go out and walk around and come back in time."

"All right but come back in time."

I was on time for the second blood extraction. Then there was a longer wait for the 3rd one, 20 or 25 minutes. I walked out on the street. Nothing much was happening. I went into a drugstore and read a magazine. I put it down, looked at the clock and went outside. I saw this woman sitting at the bus stop. She was one of those rare ones. She was showing plenty of leg. I couldn't keep my eyes off her. I crossed the street and stood about 20 yards away.

Then she got up. I had to follow her. That big ass beckoned me. I was hypnotized. She walked into a post office and I walked in behind her. She stood in a long line and I stood behind her. She got 2 postcards. I bought 12 airmail postcards and two dollars worth of stamps.

When I came out she was getting on the bus. I saw the

last of that delicious leg and ass get on the bus and the bus carried her away.

The doctor was waiting.

"What happened? You're 5 minutes late!"

"I don't know. The clock must have been wrong."

"THIS THING MUST BE EXACT!"

"Go ahead. Take the blood anyhow."

He stuck the needle into me . . .

A COUPLE of days later, the tests said there was nothing wrong with me. I didn't know if it was the 5 minutes difference or what. But the dizzy spells got worse. I began to clock out after 4 hours work without filling out. the proper forms.

I'd walk in around 11 p.m. and there would be Fay. Poor pregnant Fay.

"What happened?"

"I couldn't take any more," I'd say, "too sensitive . . ."

# 11

THE BOYS ON Dorsey station didn't know my problems.

I'd enter through the back way each night, hide my sweater in a tray and walk in to get my timecard:

"Brothers and sisters!" I'd say.

"Brother, Hank!"

"Hello, Brother Hank!"

We had a game going, the black-white game and they liked to play it. Boyer would walk up to me, touch me on the arm and say, "Man, if I had *your* paint job I'd be a millionaire!"

"Sure you would, Boyer. That's all it takes: a white skin."

Then round little Hadley would walk up to us.

"There used to be this black cook on this ship. He was the only black man aboard. He cooked tapioca pudding 2 or 3 times a week and then jacked-off into it. Those white boys really liked his tapioca pudding, hehehehe! They asked him how he made it and he said he had his own secret recipe, hehehehehehe!"

We all laughed. I don't know how many times I had to hear the tapioca pudding story . . .

"HEY, POOR white trash! Hey, boy!"

"Look, man, if I called you 'boy' you might draw steel on me. So don't call me 'boy.'"

"Look, white man, what do you say we go out together this Saturday night? I got me a nice white gal with blonde hair."

"And I got myself a nice black gal. And you know what color her hair is."

"You guys been fucking our women for centuries. We're trying to catch up. You don't mind if I stick my big black dick into your white gal?"

"If she wants it she can have it."

"You stole the land from the Indians."

"Sure I did."

"You won't invite me to your house. If you do, you'll ask me to come in the back way, so no one will see my skin . . ."

"But I'll leave a small light burning."

It got boring but there was no way out.

# 12

FAY WAS ALL right with the pregnancy. For an old gal, she was all right. We waited around at our place. Finally the time came.

"It won't be long," she said. "I don't want to get there too early."

I went out and checked the car. Came back.

"Oooh, oh," she said. "No, wait."

Maybe she *could* save the world, I was proud of her calm. I forgave her for the dirty dishes and the *New Yorker* and her writers' workshop. The old gal was only another lonely creature in a world that didn't care.

"We better go now," I said.

"No," said Fay, "I don't want to make you wait too long. I know you haven't been feeling well."

"To hell with me. Let's make it."

"No, please, Hank."

She just sat there.

"What can I do for you?" I asked.

"Nothing."

She sat there ten minutes. I went into the kitchen for a glass of water. When I came out she said, "You ready to drive?"

"Sure."

"You know where the hospital is?"

"Of course."

I helped her into the car. I had made two practice runs the week earlier. But when we got there I had no idea where to park. Fay pointed up a runway.

"Go in there. Park in there. We'll go in from there."

"Yes, mam," I said . . .

SHE WAS in bed in a back room overlooking the street. Her face grimaced. "Hold my hand," she said.

I did.

"Is it really going to happen?" I asked.

"Yes."

"You make it seem so easy," I said.

"You're so very nice. It helps."

"I'd like to *be* nice. It's that god damned post office . . ."

"I know. I know."

We were looking out the back window.

I said, "Look at those people down there. They have no idea what is going on up here. They just walk on the sidewalk. Yet, it's funny . . . they were once born themselves, each one of them."

"Yes, it is funny."

I could feel the movements of her body through her hand.

"Hold tighter," she said.

"Yes."

"I'll hate it when you go."

"Where's the doctor? Where is everybody? What the hell?"

"They'll be here."

Just then a nurse walked in. It was a Catholic hospital and she was a very handsome nurse, dark, Spanish or Portuguese.

"You . . . must go . . . now," she told me.

I gave Fay crossed fingers and a twisted smile. I don't think she saw. I took the elevator downstairs.

# 13

MY GERMAN DOCTOR walked up. The one who had given me the blood tests.

"Congratulations," he said, shaking my hand, "it's a girl. 9 pounds, 3 ounces."

"And the mother?"

"The mother will be all right. She was no trouble at all."

"When can I see them?"

"They'll let you know. Just sit there and they'll call you."

Then he was gone.

I LOOKED through the glass. The nurse pointed down at my child. The child's face was very red and it was screaming louder than any of the other children. The room was full of screaming babies. So many births! The nurse seemed very proud of my baby. At least, I hoped it was mine. She picked the girl up so I could see better. I smiled through the glass, I didn't know how to act. The girl just screamed at me. Poor thing, I thought, poor little damned thing. I didn't know then that she would be a beautiful girl someday who would look just like me, hahaha.

I motioned the nurse to put the child down, then waved goodbye to both of them. She was a nice nurse. Good legs, good hips. Fair breasts.

FAY HAD a spot of blood on the left side of her mouth and I took a wet cloth and wiped it off. Women were meant to suffer; no wonder they asked for constant declarations of love.

"I wish they'd give me my baby," said Fay, "it's not right to separate us like this."

"I know. But I guess there's some medical reason."

"Yes, but it doesn't seem right."

"No, it doesn't. But the child looked fine. I'll do what I can to make them send up the child as soon as possible. There must have been 40 babies down there. They're making all the mothers wait. I guess it's to let them get their strength back. Our baby looked *very* strong, I assure you. Please don't worry."

"I'd be so happy with my baby."

"I know, I know. It won't be long."

"Sir," a fat Mexican nurse walked up, "I'll have to ask you to leave now."

"But I'm the father."

"We know. But your wife must rest."

I squeezed Fay's hand, kissed her on the forehead. She closed her eyes and seemed to sleep then. She was not a young woman. Maybe she hadn't saved the world but she had made a major improvement. Ring one up for Fay.

# 14

MARINA LOUISE, FAY named the child. So there it was, Marina Louise Chinaski. In the crib by the window. Looking up at the tree leaves and bright designs whirling on the ceiling. Then she'd cry. Walk the baby, talk to the baby. The girl wanted mama's breasts but mama wasn't always ready and I didn't have mama's breasts. And the job was still there. And now riots. One tenth of the city was on fire . . .

# 15

ON THE ELEVATOR up, I was the only white man there. It seemed strange. They talked about the riots, not looking at me.

"Jesus," said a coal black guy, "it's really something. These guys walking around the streets drunk with 5ths of whiskey in their hands. Cops driving by but the cops don't get out of their cars, they don't bother the drunks. It's daylight. People walking around with t.v. sets, vacuum cleaners, all that. It's really something . . ."

"Yeah, man."

"The black-owned places put up signs, 'BLOOD BROTHERS.' And the white-owned places too. But they can't fool the people. They know which places belong to Whitey . . ."

"Yeah, brother."

Then the elevator stopped at the 4th floor and we all got off together. I felt that it was best for me not to make any comment at that time.

Not much later the postmaster of the city came on over the intercoms:

"Attention! The southeast area has been barricaded. Only those with proper identification will be allowed through. There is a 7 p.m. curfew. After 7 p.m. nobody will be allowed to pass. The barricade extends from Indiana Street to Hoover Street, and from Washington Boulevard to 135th Place. Anybody living in this area is excused from work now."

I got up and reached for my timecard.

"Hey! Where you going?" the supervisor asked me.

"You heard the announcement?"

"Yeah, but you're not—"

I slipped my left hand into my pocket.

"I'm not WHAT? I'm not WHAT?"

He looked at me.

"What do *you* know, WHITEY?" I said.

I took my timecard, walked over and punched out.

# 16

The riots ended, the baby calmed down, and I found ways to avoid Janko. But the dizzy spells persisted. The doctor wrote me a standing order for the green-white librium capsules and they helped a bit.

One night I got up to get a drink of water. Then I

came back, worked 30 minutes and took my ten minute break.

When I sat down again, Chambers the supervisor, a high yellow came running up:

"Chinaski! You've finally hung yourself! You've been gone 40 minutes!"

Chambers had fallen on the floor in a fit one night, frothing and twitching. They had carried him out on a stretcher. The next night he had come back, necktie, new shirt, as if nothing had happened. Now he was pulling the old water fountain game on me.

"Look, Chambers, try to be sensible. I got a drink of water, sat down, worked 30 minutes, then took my break. I was gone ten minutes."

"You've hung yourself, Chinaski! You've been gone 40 minutes! I have 7 witnesses!"

"7 witnesses?"

"YES, 7!"

"I tell you, it was ten minutes."

"No, we've got you Chinaski! We've really got you this time!"

Then, I was tired of it. I didn't want to look at him anymore:

"All right, then. I've been gone 40 minutes. Have your way. Write it up."

Chambers ran off.

I stuck a few more letters, then the general foreman walked up. A thin white man with little tufts of grey hair hanging over each ear. I looked at him and then turned and stuck some more letters.

"Mr. Chinaski, I'm sure that you understand the rules and regulations of the post office. Each clerk is allowed 2 ten minute breaks, one before lunch, the other after lunch. The break privilege is granted by management: ten minutes. Ten minutes is—"

"GOD DAMN IT!" I threw my letters down. "Now I admitted to a 40 minute break just to satisfy you guys and get you off my ass. But you keep coming around! Now I take it back! I only took 10 minutes! I want to see your 7 witnesses! Trot them out!"

Two days later I was at the racetrack. I looked up and saw all these teeth, this big smile and the eyes shining, friendly. What was it with all those teeth? I looked closer. It was Chambers looking at me, smiling and standing in a coffee line. I had a beer in my hand. I walked over to a trashcan, and still looking at him, I spit. Then I walked off. Chambers never bothered me again.

# 17

THE BABY WAS crawling, discovering the world. Marina slept in bed with us at night. There was Marina, Fay, the cat and myself. The cat slept on the bed too. Look here, I thought, I have three mouths depending on me. How very strange. I sat there and watched them sleeping.

Then two nights in a row when I came home in the mornings, the early mornings, Fay was sitting up reading the classified sections.

"All these rooms are so damned expensive," she said.

"Sure," I said.

The next night, I asked her as she read the paper:

"Are you moving out?"

"Yes."

"All right. I'll help you find a place tomorrow. I'll drive you around."

I agreed to pay her a sum each month. She said, "All right."

Fay got the girl. I got the cat.

WE FOUND a place 8 or 10 blocks away. I helped her move in, said goodbye to the girl and drove on back.

I went over to see Marina 2 or 3 or 4 times a week. I knew as long as I could see the girl I would be all right.

Fay was still wearing black to protest the war. She attended local peace demonstrations, love-ins, went to poetry readings, workshops, communist party meetings, and sat in a hippie coffee house. She took the child with her. If she wasn't out she was sitting in a chair smoking cigarette after cigarette and reading. She wore protest buttons on her black blouse. But she was usually off somewhere with the girl when I drove over to visit.

I finally found them in one day. Fay was eating sunflower seeds with yogurt. She baked her own bread but it wasn't very good.

"I met Andy, this truckdriver," she told me. "He paints on the side. That's one of his paintings." Fay pointed to the wall.

I was playing with the girl. I looked at the painting. I didn't say anything.

"He has a big cock," said Fay. "He was over the other night and he asked me, 'How would you like to be fucked with a big cock?' and I told him, 'I would rather be fucked with love!'"

"He sounds like a man of the world," I told her.

I played with the girl a little more, then left. I had a scheme test coming up.

Soon after, I got a letter from Fay. She and the child were living in a hippie commune in New Mexico. It was a nice place, she said. Marina would be able to breathe there. She enclosed a little drawing the girl had made for me.

# V

## 1

## POST OFFICE DEPARTMENT

SUBJECT: Letter of Warning

TO: Mr. Henry Chinaski

Information has been received in this office indicating that you were arrested by the Los Angeles Police Department on March 12, 1969, on a drunk charge.

In this connection, your attention is invited to Section 744.12 of the Postal Manual, as follows:

"Postal employees are servants of the general public and their conduct, in many instances, must be subject to more restrictions and to higher standards than may be for certain private employments. Employees are expected to conduct themselves during and outside of working hours in a manner which will reflect favorably upon the Postal Service. Although it is not the policy of the Post Office Department to interfere with the private lives of employees, it does require that Postal personnel be honest,

reliable, trustworthy, and of good character and reputa-
tion."

While your arrest was on a relatively minor charge, it
constitutes evidence of your failure to conduct yourself as
required in a manner which will reflect favorably upon the
Postal Service. You are hereby cautioned and warned that
a repetition of this offense or other involvement with
police authorities will leave this office no alternative but to
consider disciplinary action.

You may submit your written explanation in this matter
if you wish to do so.

# 2

## POST OFFICE DEPARTMENT

SUBJECT: Notice of Proposed Adverse Action

TO: Mr. Henry Chinaski

This is advance notice that it is proposed to suspend you
from duty without pay for 3 days or to take such other
disciplinary action as may be determined to be appropriate.
The proposed action is considered to be for such cause as
will promote the efficiency of the service and will be
effected no sooner than 35 calendar days from the receipt
of this letter.

The charge against you and the reasons supporting the
charge are:

*CHARGE NO.* 1

You are charged with being absent without leave on May 13, 1969, May 14, 1969, and May 15, 1969.

In addition to the above, the following element of your past record will be considered in determining the extent of disciplinary action should the current charge be sustained:

You were issued a letter of warning April 1, 1969, for being absent without leave.

You have a right to answer the charge in person or in writing, or both, and to be accompanied by a representative of your own choosing. Your reply is to be made within ten (10) calendar days of the receipt of this letter. You may also submit affidavits in support of your answer. Any written reply should be directed to the Postmaster, Los Angeles, California 90052. If additional time is needed within which to submit your reply, it will be considered upon written application showing the necessity.

If you wish to reply in person, you may make an appointment with Ellen Normell, Chief Employment and Services Section, or K. T. Shamus, Employee Services Officer, by telephoning 289-2222.

After the expiration of the 10-day time limit for reply, all of the facts in your case, including any reply you may submit, will be given full consideration before a decision is rendered. A decision in writing will be issued to you. If the decision is adverse, the letter of decision will advise you of the reason, or reasons, relied upon in making the decision.

# 3

## POST OFFICE DEPARTMENT

SUBJECT: Notice of Decision

TO: Henry Chinaski

This will refer to the letter addressed to you dated August 17, 1969, proposing your suspension without pay for three days or other disciplinary action, based on Charge No. 1 specified therein. To date no reply has been received to that letter. After careful consideration of the charge, it has been decided that Charge No. 1, which is supported by substantial evidence, is sustained and warrants your suspension. Accordingly, you will be suspended from duty without pay for a period of three (3) days.

Your first day of suspension will be November 17, 1969, and your last day of suspension will be November 19, 1969.

The element of your past record, as set forth in detail in the letter of proposed adverse action, was also considered in deciding upon the penalty to be imposed.

You have the right to appeal this decision either to the Post Office Department or to the U.S. Civil Service Commission, or first to the Post Office Department and then to the Civil Service Department and then to the Civil Service Commission, in accordance with the following:

If you appeal first to the Civil Service Commission, you will have no right to appeal to the Post Office Department.

An appeal to the Civil Service Commission must be submitted to the Regional Director, San Francisco Region, U.S. Civil Service Commission, 450 Golden Gate Avenue, Box 36010, San Francisco, California 94102. Your appeal must (a) be in writing, (b) set forth your reasons for contesting the suspension, with such offer of proof and documents as you are able to submit, and (c) be submitted no later than 15 days after the effective date of your suspension. The Commission will upon proper appeal, review the action only to determine that, proper procedures have been followed, unless you furnish an affidavit alleging that the action is for political reasons, except as may be required by law, or resulted from discrimination because of marital status or physical handicap.

If you appeal to the Post Office Department, you will not be entitled to appeal to the Commission until after a first level decision has been made on your appeal by the Department. At that point, you will have a choice of continuing with your appeal through higher levels in the Post Office Department or appealing to the Commission. However, if no first level decision on the appeal has been made within 60 days after it is filed, you may elect to terminate your appeal to the Department by appealing to the Commission.

If you appeal to the Post Office Department within ten (10) calendar days of receiving this notice of decision, your suspension will not be put into effect until you have received a decision on your appeal from the Regional Director, Post Office Department. Further, if you appeal to the Department, you have the right to be accompanied, represented, and advised by a representative of your own choosing. You and your representative will have freedom from restraint, interference, coercion, discrimination, or reprisal. You and your representative will also be allowed a reasonable amount of official time to prepare your presentation.

An appeal to the Post Office Department may be submitted at any time after you receive this letter but not later than 15 calendar days after the effective date of the suspension. Your letter must include a request for a hearing or a statement that no hearing is desired. The appeal should be addressed to:

Regional Director
Post Office Department
631 Howard Street
San Francisco, California
94106

If you file an appeal with either the Regional Director or with the Civil Service Commission, furnish me with a signed copy of the appeal at the same time it is sent to the Region or Civil Service Commission.

If you have any questions about the appeals procedure, you may contact Richard N. Marth, Employee Services and Benefits Assistant, at the Employment and Services Section, Office of Personnel, Room 2205, Federal Building, 300 North Los Angeles Street, between 8:30 a.m. and 4 p.m., Monday through Friday.

# 4

## POST OFFICE DEPARTMENT

SUBJECT: Notice of Proposed Adverse Action

TO: Henry Chinaski

This is advance notice that it is proposed to remove you from the Postal Service or to take such other disciplinary action as may be determined to be appropriate. The proposed action is considered to be for such cause as will promote the efficiency of the service and will be affective no sooner than 35 calendar days from the receipt of this letter.

The charge against you and the reasons supporting the charge are:

*CHARGE NO.* 1

You are charged with being absent without leave on the following dates:

September 25, 1969 4 hrs
September 28, 1969 8 hrs
September 29, 1969 8 hrs
October 5, 1969 8 hrs
October 6, 1969 4 hrs
October 7, 1969 4 hrs
October 13, 1969 5 hrs
October 15, 1969 4 hrs
October 16, 1969 8 hrs
October 19, 1969 8 hrs
October 23, 1969 4 hrs
October 29, 1969 4 hrs
November 4, 1969 8 hrs
November 6, 1969 4 hrs
November 12, 1969 4 hrs
November 13, 1969 8 hrs

In addition to the above, the following elements of your past record will be considered in determining the extent of disciplinary action should the current charge be sustained:

You were issued with a letter of warning April 1, 1969, for being absent without leave.

You were issued a notice of proposed adverse action August 17, 1969, for being absent without leave. As a result of that charge you were suspended from duty without pay for three days from November 17, 1969 to November 19, 1969.

You have the right to answer the charge in person or in writing, or both, and to be accompanied by a representative of your own choosing. Your reply is to be made within ten (10) calendar days of the receipt of this letter. You may also submit affidavits in support of your answers. Any written reply should be directed to the Postmaster, Los Angeles, California 90052. If additional time is needed within which to submit your reply, it will be considered upon written application showing the necessity.

If you wish to reply in person, you may make an appointment with Ellen Normell, Chief, Employment and Services Section, or K. T. Shamus, Employee Services Officer, by telephoning 289-2222.

After the expiration of the 10-day limit for reply, all of the facts in your case, including any reply you may submit, will be given full consideration before a decision is rendered. A decision in writing will be issued to you. If the decision is adverse, the letter of decision will advise you of the reason, or reasons, relied upon in making the decision.

# VI

## 1

I WAS SITTING next to a young girl who didn't know her scheme very well.

"Where does 2900 Roteford go?" she asked me.

"Try throwing it to 33," I told her.

The supervisor was talking to her.

"You say you're from Kansas City? Both my parents were born in Kansas City."

"Is that so?" said the girl.

Then she asked me:

"How about 8400 Meyers?"

"Give it to 18."

She was a little on the plump side but she was ready. I passed. I'd had it with the ladies for a while.

The supervisor was standing real close to her.

"Do you live far from work?"

"No."

"Do you like your job?"

"Oh, yes."

She turned to me:

"How about 6200 Albany?"

"16."

When I finished my tray, the supervisor spoke to me:

"Chinaski, I timed you on that tray. It took you 28 minutes."

I didn't answer.

"Do you know what the standard is for that tray?"

"No, I don't know."

"How long have you been here?"

"Eleven years."

"You've been here eleven years and you don't know the standard?"

"That's correct."

"You stick mail as if you don't care about it."

The girl still had a full tray in front of her. We had begun our trays together.

"And you've been talking to this lady next to you."

I lit a cigarette.

"Chinaski, come here a minute."

He stood at the front of the tin cases and pointed. All the clerks were sticking very fast now. I watched them swinging their right arms frantically. Even the plump girl was jamming them home.

"See these numbers painted on the end of the case?"

"Yeh."

"Those numbers indicate the number of pieces that must be stuck in a minute. A 2 foot tray must be stuck in 23 minutes. You ran 5 minutes over."

He pointed to the 23. "23 minutes is standard."

"That 23 doesn't mean anything," I said.

"Whadda ya mean?"

"I mean a man came along and painted that 23 on there with a can of paint."

"No, no, this is time-tested over the years and rechecked."

What was the use? I didn't answer.

"I'm going to have to write you up, Chinaski. You will be counseled on this."

I went back and sat down. 11 years! I didn't have a dime more in my pocket than when I had first walked in. 11 years. Although each night had been long, the years had gone fast. Perhaps it was the night work. Or doing the same thing over and over and over again. At least with The Stone I had never known what to expect. Here there weren't any surprises.

11 years shot through the head. I had seen the job eat men up. They seemed to melt. There was Jimmy Potts of Dorsey Station. When I first came in, Jimmy had been a well-built guy in a white T shirt. Now he was gone. He put his seat as close to the floor as possible and braced himself from falling over with his feet. He was too tired to get a haircut and had worn the same pair of pants for 3 years. He changed shirts twice a week and he walked very slow. They had murdered him. He was 55. He had 7 years to go until retirement.

"I'll never make it," he told me.

They either melted or they got fat, huge, especially around the ass and the belly. It was the stool and the same motion and the same talk. And there I was, dizzy spells and pains in the arms, neck, chest, everywhere. I slept all day resting up for the job. On weekends I had to drink in order to forget it. I had come in weighing 185 pounds. Now I weighed 223 pounds. All you moved was your right arm.

## 2

I WALKED INTO the counselor's office. It was Eddie Beaver sitting behind the desk. The clerks called him "Skinny Beaver." He had a pointed head, pointed nose, pointed chin. He was all points. And out for them too.

"Sit down, Chinaski."

Beaver had some papers in his hand. He read them.

"Chinaski, it took you 28 minutes to throw a 23 minute tray."

"Oh, knock off the bullshit. I'm tired."

"What?"

"I said, knock off the bullshit! Let me sign the paper and go back. I don't want to hear it all."

"I'm here to counsel you, Chinaski!"

I sighed. "O.K., go ahead. Let's hear it."

"We have a production schedule to meet, Chinaski."

"Yeh."

"And when you fall behind on production that means that somebody else is going to stick your mail for you. That means overtime."

"You mean *I* am responsible for those 3 and one half hours overtime they call almost every night?"

"Look, you took 28 minutes on a 23 minute tray. That's all there is to it."

"You know better. Each tray is 2 feet long. Some trays have 3, or even 4 times as many letters than others. The clerks grab what they call the 'fat' trays. I don't bother. Somebody has to stick with the tough mail. Yet all you guys know is that each tray is two feet long and that it must be stuck in 23 minutes. But we're not sticking trays in those cases, we're sticking letters."

"No, no, this thing has been time-tested!"

"Maybe it has. I doubt it. But if you're going to time a man, don't judge him on *one* tray. Even Babe Ruth struck out now and then. Judge a man on ten trays, or a night's work. You guys just use this thing to hang anybody who gets in your craw."

"All right, you've had your say, Chinaski. Now, I'm telling YOU: you stuck a 28 minute tray. *We* go by that.

145

NOW, if you are caught on another slow tray you will be due for ADVANCED COUNSELING!"

"All right, just let me ask you one question?"

"All right."

"Suppose I get an easy tray. Once in a while I do. Sometimes I finish a tray in 5 minutes or in 8 minutes. Let's say I stick a tray in 8 minutes. According to the time-tested standard I have saved the post office 15 minutes. Now can I take these 15 minutes and go down to the cafeteria, have a slice of pie with ice cream, watch t.v. and come back?"

"No! YOU ARE SUPPOSED TO GRAB A TRAY IMMEDIATELY AND START STICKING MAIL!"

I signed a paper saying that I had been counseled. Then Skinny Beaver signed my travel form, wrote the time on it and sent me back to my stool to stick more mail.

## 3

BUT, THERE WERE still bits of action. One guy was caught on the same stairway that I had been trapped on. He was caught there with his head under some girl's skirt. Then one of the girls who worked in the cafeteria complained that she hadn't been paid, as promised, for a bit of oral copulation she had supplied to a general foreman and 3 mailhandlers. They fired the girl and the 3 mailhandlers and busted the general foreman down to supervisor.

Then, I set the post office on fire.

I had been sent to fourth class papers and was smoking a cigar, working a stack of mail off of a hand truck when some guy come by and said, "HEY, YOUR MAIL IS ON FIRE!"

I looked around. There it was. A small flame was starting to stand up like a dancing snake. Evidently part of a burning cigar ash had fallen in there earlier.

"Oh shit!"

The flame grew rapidly. I took a catalogue and, holding it flat, I beat the shit out of it. Sparks flew. It was hot. As soon as I put out one section, another caught up.

I heard a voice:

"Hey! I smell fire!"

"YOU DON'T SMELL FIRE," I yelled, "YOU SMELL SMOKE!"

"I think I'm going to get out of here!"

"God damn you, then," I screamed, "GET OUT!"

The flames were burning my hands. I *had* to save the United States mail, 4th class junkmail!

Finally, I got it under control. I took my foot and pushed the whole pile of papers onto the floor and stepped on the last bit of red ash.

The supervisor walked up to say something to me. I stood there with the burned catalogue in my hand and waited. He looked at me and walked off.

Then I resumed casing the 4th class junkmail. Anything burned, I put to one side.

My cigar had gone out. I didn't light it again.

My hands began to hurt and I walked over to the water fountain, put them under water. It didn't help.

I found the supervisor and asked him for a travel slip to the nurse's office.

It was the same one who used to come to my door and ask me, "Now what's the matter, Mr. Chinaski?"

When I walked in, she said the same thing again.

"You remember me, eh?" I asked.

"Oh yes, I know you've had some real sick nights."

"Yeh," I said.

147

"Do you still have women up at your apartment?" she asked.

"Yeh. Do you still have men up at yours?"

"All right, Mr. Chinaski, now what's your problem?"

"I burned my hands."

"Come over here. How did you burn your hands?"

"Does it matter? They're burned."

She was dabbing my hands with something. One of her breasts brushed me.

"How did it happen, Henry?"

"Cigar. I was standing next to a truck of 4th class. Ash must have gotten in there. Flames came up."

The breast was up against me again.

"Hold your hands still, *please!*"

Then she laid her whole flank against me as she spread some ointment on my hands. I was sitting on a stool.

"What's the matter, Henry? You seem nervous."

"Well . . . you know how it is, Martha."

"My name is *not* Martha. It's Helen."

"Let's get married, Helen."

"What?"

"I mean, how soon will I be able to use my hands again?"

"You can use them right now if you feel like it."

"What?"

"I mean, on the work floor."

She wrapped on some gauze.

"You mustn't burn the mails."

"It was junk."

"All mail is important."

"All right, Helen."

She walked over to her desk and I followed her. She filled out the travel form. She looked very cute in her little white hat. I'd have to find a way to get back there.

She saw me looking at her body.

"All right, Mr. Chinaski, I think you better leave now."

"Oh yes . . . Well, thanks for everything."

"It's just part of the job."

"Sure."

A week later there were NO SMOKING IN THIS AREA signs all around. The clerks were not allowed to smoke unless they used ashtrays. Somebody had been contracted to manufacture all these ashtrays. They were nice. And said PROPERTY OF THE UNITED STATES GOVERNMENT. The clerks stole most of them.

NO SMOKING.

I had all by myself, Henry Chinaski, revolutionized the postal system.

# 4

THEN SOME MEN came around and ripped out every other water-fountain.

"Hey, look, look what the hell are they doing?" I asked.

Nobody seemed interested.

I was in the 3rd class flat section. I walked over to another clerk.

"Look!" I said. "They are taking away our water!"

He glanced at the waterfountain, then went back to sticking his 3rd class.

I tried other clerks. They showed the same disinterest. I couldn't understand it.

I asked to have my union representative paged to my area.

After a long delay, here he came—Parker Anderson. Parker used to sleep in an old used car and freshen up and shave and shit at gas stations that didn't lock their restrooms. Parker had tried to be a hustler but had failed. And had come to the central post office, joined the union, and went to the union meetings where he became sarge-at-arms. He was soon a union representative, and then he was elected vice president.

"What's the matter, Hank? I know you don't need *me* to handle these soups!"

"Don't butter me, babe. Now I've been paying union dues for almost 12 years and haven't asked for a damn thing."

"All right, what's wrong?"

"It's the waterfountains."

"The waterfountains are wrong?"

"No, god damn it, the waterfountains are right. It's what they are doing to them. Look."

"Look? Where?"

"*There!*"

"I don't see anything."

"That's the exact nature of my bitch. There used to be a waterfountain there."

"So they took it out. What the hell?"

"Look, Parker, I wouldn't mind one. But they are yanking out every *other* waterfountain in the building. If we don't stop them here, they will soon be closing down every other crapper . . . and then, what next, I don't know . . ."

"All right," said Parker, "what do you want me to do?"

"I want you to get off your ass and find out why these waterfountains are being removed."

"All right, I'll see you tomorrow."

"See that you do. 12 years worth of union dues is $312."

THE NEXT day I had to look for Parker. He didn't have the answer. Or the next or the next. I told Parker that I was tired of waiting. He had one more day.

The next day he came up to me in the coffee break area.

"All right, Chinaski, I found out."

"Yes?"

"In 1912 when this building was built . . ."

"1912? That's over a half century ago! No wonder this place looks like the Kaiser's whorehouse!"

"All right, stop it. Now, in 1912 when this place was built, the contract called for a *certain* number of waterfountains. In checking, the p.o. found that there had been *twice* as many waterfountains installed as were called for in the original contract."

"Well, o.k.," I said, "what harm can twice as many waterfountains do? The clerks will only drink so much water."

"Right. But the waterfountains happen to jut out a bit. They get in the way."

"So?"

"All right. Supposing a clerk with a sharp lawyer was injured against a waterfountain? Say he was pinned against the fountain by a handtruck loaded with heavy sacks of magazines?"

"I see it now. The fountain isn't supposed to be there. The post office is sued for negligence."

"Right!"

"All right. Thanks, Parker."

"My service."

If he had made up the story, it was damn near worth $312. I'd seen a lot worse printed in *Playboy*.

## 5

I FOUND THAT the only way I could keep from dizzy-spelling into my case was to get up and take a walk now and then.

Fazzio, a supervisor who had the station at the time, saw me walking up to one of the rare waterfountains.

"Look, Chinaski, everytime I see you, you're walking!"

"That's nothing," I said, "everytime I see you, you're walking."

"But that's part of my job. Walking is part of my job. I have to do it."

"Look," I said, "it's part of my job too. I have to do it. If I stay on that stool much longer I am going to leap up on top of those tin cases and start running around whistling *Dixie* from my asshole and *Mammy's Little Children Love Shortnin' Bread* through the frontal orifice."

"All right, Chinaski, forget it."

# 6

ONE NIGHT I was coming around the corner after sneaking down to the cafeteria for a pack of smokes. And there was a face I knew.

It was Tom Moto! The guy I had subbed with under The Stone!

"Moto, you motherfuck!" I said.

"Hank!" he said.

We shook hands.

"Hey, I was thinking of you! Jonstone is retiring this month. Some of us are holding a farewell party for him. You know, he always liked to fish. We're going to take him out in a rowboat. Maybe you'd like to come along and throw him overboard, drown him. We've got a nice deep lake."

"No, shit, I just don't even want to look at him."

"But you're *invited*."

Moto was grinning from asshole to eyebrow. Then I looked at his shirt: a supervisor's badge.

"Oh no, Tom."

"Hank, I've got 4 kids. They need me for bread and butter."

"All right, Tom," I said.

Then I walked off.

7

I DON'T KNOW how it happens to people. I had child support, need for something to drink, rent, shoes, shirts, socks, all that stuff. Like everyone else I needed an old car, something to eat, all the little intangibles.

Like women.

Or a day at the track.

With everything on the line and no way out, you don't even think about it.

I parked across the street from the Federal Building and stood waiting for the signal to change. I walked across. Pushed through the swinging doors. It was as if I were a piece of iron drawn to the magnet. There was nothing I could do.

It was on the 2nd floor. I opened the door and they were in there. The clerks of the Federal Building. I noticed one girl, poor thing, only one arm. She'd be there forever. It was like being an old wino like me. Well, as the boys said, you had to work somewhere. So they accepted what there was. This was the wisdom of the slave.

A young black girl walked up. She was well-dressed and pleased with her surroundings. I was happy for her. I would have gone mad with the same job.

"Yes?" she asked.

"I'm a postal clerk," I said, "I want to resign."

She reached under the counter and came up with a stack of papers.

"All these?"

She smiled, "Sure you can do it?"

"Don't worry," I said, "I can do it."

# 8

You HAD TO fill out more papers to get out than to get in.

The first page they gave you was a personalized mimeo affair from the postmaster of the city.

It began:

"I am sorry you are terminating your position with the post office and . . . etc., etc., etc., etc."

How could he be sorry? He didn't even know me.

There was a list of questions.

"Did you find our supervisors understanding? Were you able to relate to them?"

Yes, I answered.

"Did you find the supervisors in any manner prejudiced toward race, religion, background or any related factor?"

No, I answered.

Then there was one—"Would you advise your friends to seek employment in the post office?"

Of course, I answered.

"If you have any grievances or complaints about the post office please list them in detail on the reverse side of this page."

No grievances, I answered.

Then my black girl was back.

"Finished already?"

"Finished."

"I've never seen anybody fill out their papers that fast."

" 'Quickly,' " I said.

" 'Quickly'?" she asked. "What do you mean?"

"I mean, what do we do next?"

"Please step in."

I followed her ass between desks to a place almost to the back.

"Sit down," the man said.

He took some time reading through the papers. Then he looked at me.

"May I ask why you are resigning? Is it because of disciplinary procedures against you?"

"No."

"Then what is the reason for your resignation?"

"To pursue a career."

"To pursue a career?"

He looked at me. I was less than 8 months from my 50th birthday. I knew what he was thinking.

"May I ask what your 'career' will be?"

"Well, sir, I'll tell you. The trapping season in the bayou only lasts from December through February. I've already lost a month."

"A month? But you've been here eleven years."

"All right, then, I've wasted eleven years. I can pick up 10 to 20 grand for 3 months trapping at Bayou La Fourche."

"What do you do?"

"*Trap!* Muskrats, nutria, mink, otter . . . coon. All I need is a pirogue. I give 20 percent of my take for use of the land. I get paid a buck and a quarter for muskrat skins, 3 bucks for mink, 4 bucks for 'bo mink,' a buck and a half for nutria and 25 bucks for otter. I sell the muskrat carcass, which is about a foot long, for 5 cents to a cat food factory. I get 25 cents for the skinned body of the nutria. I raise pigs, chickens and ducks. I catch catfish. There's nothing to it. I—"

"Never mind, Mr. Chinaski, that will be sufficient."

155

He put some papers in his typewriter and typed away.

Then I looked up and there was Parker Anderson my union man, good old gas-station shaving and shitting Parker, giving me his politician's grin.

"You resigning, Hank? I *know* you been threatenin' to for eleven years . . ."

"Yeah, I'm going to Southern Louisiana and catch myself a batch of goodies."

"They got a racetrack down there?"

"You kidding? The Fair Grounds is one of the oldest tracks in the country!"

Parker had a young white boy with him—one of the neurotic tribe of the lost—and the kid's eyes were filmed with wet layers of tears. One big tear in each eye. They did not drop out. It was fascinating. I had seen women sit and look at me with those same eyes before they got mad and started screaming about what a son of a bitch I was. Evidently the boy had fallen into one of the many traps, and he had gone running for Parker. Parker would save his job.

The man gave me one more paper to sign and then I got out of there.

Parker said, "Luck, old man," as I walked by.

"Thanks, baby," I answered.

I didn't *feel* any different. But I knew that soon, like a man lifted quickly out of the deep sea, I would be afflicted—with a particular type of bends. I was like Joyce's damned parakeets. After living in the cage I had taken the opening and flown out—like a shot into the heavens. Heavens?

# 9

I WENT INTO the bends. I got drunker and stayed drunker than a shit skunk in Purgatory. I even had the butcher knife against my throat one night in the kitchen and then I thought, easy, old boy, your little girl might want you to take her to the zoo. Ice cream bars, chimpanzees, tigers, green and red birds, and the sun coming down on top of her head, the sun coming down and crawling into the hairs of your arms, easy, old boy.

When I came to, I was in the front room of my apartment, spitting into the rug, putting cigarettes out against my wrists, laughing. Mad as a March Hare. I looked up and there sat this pre-med student. A human heart sat in a homey fat jar between us on the coffectable. All around the human heart—which was labeled after its former owner "Francis"—were half empty fifths of whiskey and scotch, clutters of beerbottles, ashtrays, garbage. I'd pick up a bottle and swallow a hellish mixture of beer and ashes. I hadn't eaten for 2 weeks. An endless stream of people had come and gone. There had been 7 or 8 wild parties where I had kept demanding—"More to drink! More to drink! More to drink!" I was flying up to heaven; they were just talking—and fingering each other.

"Yeh," I said to the pre-med student, "what do you want with me?"

"I am going to be your own personal physician."

"All right, doctor, the first thing I want you to do is to take that god damned human heart out of here!"

"Uh uh."

"What?"

"The heart stays here."

"Look, man, I don't know your name!"

"Wilbert."

"Well, Wilbert, I don't know who you are or how you got here but you take 'Francis' with you!"

"No, it stays with you."

Then he got his little playbag and the rubber wrap-around for the arm and he squeezed the ball and the rubber inflated.

"You've got the blood pressure of a 19 year old," he told me.

"Fuck that. Look, isn't it against the law to leave human hearts laying around?"

"I'll be back to get it. Now, breathe *in!*"

"I thought the post office was driving me crazy. Now you come along."

"Quiet. Breathe *in!*"

"I need a good young piece of ass, doctor. That's what's wrong with me."

"Your backbone is out of place in 14 areas, Chinaski. That breeds tension, imbecility, and, often, madness."

"Balls!" I said . . .

I DON'T remember the gentleman leaving. I awakened on my couch at 1.10 p.m. in the afternoon, death in the afternoon, and it was hot, the sun ripping through my torn shades to rest on the jar in the center of the coffeetable. "Francis" had stayed with me all night, stewing in alcoholic brine, swimming in the mucous extension of the dead diastole. Sitting there in the jar.

It looked like fried chicken. I mean, before you fried it. Exactly.

I picked it up and put it in my closet and covered it with a torn shirt. Then I went to the bathroom and vomited. I finished, stuck my face against the mirror. There were long black hairs sticking out all over my face. Suddenly I had to sit down and shit. It was a good hot one.

The doorbell rang. I finished wiping my ass, got into some old clothes and went to the door.

"Hello?"

There was a young guy out there with long blonde hair hanging down around his face and a black girl who just kept smiling as if she were crazy.

"Hank?"

"Yeh. Who you 2 guys?"

"She is a woman. Don't you remember us? From the party? We brought a flower."

"Oh balls, come on in."

They brought in the flower, some kind of red-orange thing on a green stem. It made a lot more sense than many things, except that it had been murdered. I found a bowl, put the flower in, brought out a jug of wine and put it on the coffeetable.

"You don't remember her?" the kid asked. "You said you wanted to fuck her."

She laughed.

"Very nice, but not now."

"Chinaski, how are you going to make it without the post office?"

"I don't know. Maybe I'll fuck you. Or let you fuck me. Hell, I don't know."

"You can sleep on our floor anytime."

"Can I watch while you fuck?"

"Sure."

We drank. I had forgotten their names. I showed them the heart. I asked them to take the horrible thing with them. I didn't dare throw it out in case the pre-med student needed it back for an exam or at the expiration of the med-library loan or whatever.

So we went down and saw a nude floor show, drinking and hollering and laughing. I don't know who had the money but I think he had most of it, which was nice for a change, and I kept laughing and squeezing the girl's ass and her thighs and kissing her, but nobody cared. As long as the money lasted, you lasted.

They drove me back and he left with her. I got into the door, said goodbye, turned on the radio, found a half-pint of scotch, drank that, laughing, feeling good, finally relaxed, free, burning my fingers with short cigar butts, then made it to the bed, made it to the edge, tripped, fell down, fell down across the mattress, slept, slept, slept . . .

IN THE morning it was morning and I was still alive.

Maybe I'll write a novel, I thought.

And then I did.